Eric Malpass was born in Derby
bank after leaving school, but
become a novelist and he wrote
years. His first book, *Morning's at Seven*, was published to
wide acclaim. With an intuitive eye for the quirkiness
of family life, his novels are full of wry comments and
perceptive observations. This exquisite sense of detail has led
to the filming of three of his books. His most engaging
character is Gaylord Pentecost – a charming seven-year-old
who observes the strange adult world with utter incredulity.

Eric Malpass also wrote biographical novels, carefully
researched and highly evocative of the period. Among these is
Of Human Frailty, the moving story of Thomas Cranmer.

With his amusing and lovingly drawn details of life in
rural England, Malpass' books typify a certain whimsical
Englishness – a fact which undoubtedly contributes to his
popularity in Europe. Married with a family, Eric Malpass
lived in Long Eaton, near Nottingham, until his death in
1996.

ERIC MALPASS

MORNING'S AT SEVEN

HOUSE OF
STRATUS

This edition published in 2001 by House of Stratus, an imprint of
Stratus Books Ltd., 21 Beeching Park, Kelly Bray,
Cornwall, PL17 8QS, UK.

www.houseofstratus.com

Typeset, printed and bound by House of Stratus.

A catalogue record for this book is available from the British Library
and the Library of Congress.

ISBN 0-7551-0192-8

To Michael and Janet
Heather and Rosemary

Chapter 1

Dawn, and a cold-porridge sky. A few wet clouts of snow still lying in the angles of the roof.

In the big, rambling house the family were wrapped in Sunday morning hibernation, huddled against the cold and the coming day.

But Gaylord was impervious to cold. Young Gaylord Pentecost was impervious to almost everything. Waking, he tramped about on his bed for a bit. Tiring of this, he hitched his pyjamas about his non-existent waist, and set off on a goodwill tour of the house.

He went to see Grandpa. It was dark in Grandpa's room. He drew the curtains.

The curtains were on brass rings. Drawn by anyone they made a noise like castanets. Drawn by Gaylord they sounded like a pile-up on the M1.

Grandpa did not even open his eyes. 'Get the hell out of here,' he said.

Under the bedclothes Grandpa was a tight, round little mountain. Gaylord took a flying leap and landed on top of the mountain. 'I'm a knight,' he cried. 'And you are my charger.'

'I am not a charger,' said Grandpa. 'I am just an old man seeking a little rest. God help me.'

Gaylord put an examining finger on one ancient eyelid. He pushed it up, gazed thoughtfully at the yellow, baleful eye. He let it fall. 'Shall I make you a cup of tea?'

'If it will take a long time, yes,' said Grandpa.

Gaylord dismounted. 'Won't be two ticks,' he said cheerfully.

'Please don't hurry,' said Grandpa.

Gaylord went to see Great Aunt Marigold. 'Would you like a cup of tea?' he cried from the doorway.

But Aunt Marigold, whose hearing-aid was on the bedside table with her glasses and her teeth, Aunt Marigold lay doggo, reflecting that this was one of the occasions when her deafness ceased to be an affliction and became a blessing and a haven of refuge.

Gaylord visited Auntie Rose. Auntie Rose's long, sallow face was no more than a yellow stain on the white pillow. It remained devoid of joy at sight of her nephew. 'What are you reading?' asked Gaylord.

'A book.'

'What's it called?'

'*Psychopathology in Everyday Life*,' said Auntie Rose. 'Any wiser?' she asked nastily.

The syllables tumbled into Gaylord's brain like coal down a chute. And lay higgledy-piggledy at the bottom. He went and peered over Auntie Rose's shoulder. 'Has it got pictures?'

'No,' said Auntie Rose.

'What's it about?'

'Psychopathology,' said Auntie Rose. 'In everyday life,' she elaborated.

Gaylord gave a tentative pull at the covers. 'Can I come in?'

A sudden change came over Auntie Rose. She bunched herself up like a cornered cat. Her lips were stretched tight over her teeth. She gripped her book like a cyclist hurtling downhill without brakes. 'The one hour of the day when I can get a bit of quiet from this mad damned family, and you have to come in. Now go away and let me get on with this book. Go and see Becky. She'll enjoy having someone in her bed, even you.' She stared at the printed page, quivering.

Gaylord watched her with interest. This had happened before. You could be holding a quite normal conversation with Auntie Rose and suddenly she'd be all coiled up to spring. Very interesting. Of course, he knew what the trouble was. He'd heard Grandpa say. He went and climbed on the foot of the brass bedstead. There didn't seem much point in staying. 'Would you like a cup of tea?' he asked.

Auntie Rose didn't reply. Gaylord thought he would go and see Auntie Becky.

Auntie Becky was all pink and cream, frothy and frilly. Gaylord liked Auntie Becky. He had pretty well decided to marry her when he grew up. He gave a tentative tug at *her* bedclothes. 'Hop in,' said Auntie Becky.

He hopped in. Auntie Becky was warm, and soft, and smelt nice. Gaylord was neither warm nor soft. It was like having a large frog in bed, she thought. 'What have you been doing?' she asked.

'Been to see Auntie Rose.'

'What was she doing?'

'Reading.'

Auntie Becky sounded amused. 'What?'

Gaylord looked at the pile of syllables. Psych — 'Something about cycling,' he hazarded.

'Good Lord.'

'And then she went all funny.'

'Funny?'

'All screwed up. I don't think she wanted me to stay much.'

'Poor Rose,' Becky said with lazy satisfaction.

Gaylord thought it was time to trot out Grandpa's diagnosis. 'It's her goddam noives,' he said.

Auntie Becky threw back her head and laughed. Gaylord saw between her white teeth her little pink tongue. He put in a finger and touched it. 'What have you been doing?' he asked.

'Dreaming.'

'What about?'

'Men,' said Auntie Becky, stretching contentedly.

It seemed a dull thing to dream about. 'Would you like a cup of tea?' he asked.

'I'd love one.'

Gaylord climbed out, took another hitch at his pyjamas, and made for the door. 'Shan't be two ticks,' he said. He went to see Momma and Poppa.

He was intrigued to find Momma in bed alone. 'Momma, where's Poppa?' he asked.

'In the attic,' said Momma.

Gaylord went and shoved things about on the dressing table. 'Why is Poppa in the attic, Momma?' he asked.

'Because he is a low-down heel and we failed to see eye to eye,' said Momma.

'What about did you fail to see eye to eye?' asked Gaylord.

'Money,' said Momma.

Gaylord trundled up to the attic. Poppa was lying on the camp bed, wrapped untidily in army blankets like an Egyptian mummy coming undone. Desperately he feigned sleep. 'Why are you sleeping in the attic, Poppa?' asked Gaylord.

'I am not,' said Poppa. 'I was, but I was rudely awakened.'

Subtle rebuke was one of the things Gaylord was impervious to. 'I should have thought it was cold in the attic,' he said.

'It is,' said Poppa. 'Bloody cold.'

'Momma looked ever so cosy,' Gaylord said. 'Would you like a cup of tea?'

'Please,' said Poppa. He turned his face to the wall. Gaylord set off on his errand of mercy. Down in the kitchen he turned the cold tap on full. Then he put his finger over the hole. The water squirted deliciously over the kitchen and over Gaylord. He looked at his wet pyjamas, and mentally crossed Momma off the tea list. He was developing a sixth sense as to what Momma would go on about. He didn't really care much for Momma. All too often they failed to see eye to eye.

He found an assortment of cups and saucers, set them out on a tray, half filled them with a saturated solution of milk and sugar. Then he filled the half gallon kettle and put it on the gas to boil.

It took a long time. Gaylord grew bored. Momma had told him about a little boy who had held a spoon over the spout of a boiling kettle and invented railway engines. When the kettle eventually boiled he tried it. The lid shot off. Gaylord couldn't quite see what it had to do with railway engines, but decided he'd invent something himself one day, except that railway engines had already been invented, and he couldn't think of anything else to invent, which seemed to make it difficult.

He tipped a quarter of tea into the pot. Being a cautious child he turned off the gas and let the kettle cool off a bit before he poured. But at last all was ready. He filled up the cups. There were so many tea leaves floating on top that the result looked more like grey mint sauce than tea, but he didn't suppose it would matter. He plodded upstairs with the tray.

He took a cup in to Grandpa. Grandpa looked at the hell brew and shuddered. 'I'll just leave it to cool,' he said.

'It *is* cool,' said Gaylord.

He went over to the window and looked out. The November day was frore. Like a patient who breathes but does not see or move or feel, it would stay just alive until the winter's dusk seeped mercifully into the countryside. Then it would die; unloved, unmourned, almost unnoticed. 'Poppa didn't sleep with Momma,' said Gaylord.

'More fool him,' said Grandpa.

Gaylord took the glad news to Great Aunt Marigold. Despite her deafness, Great Aunt Marigold had a knack of cottoning on to anything that interested her. Now she jerked up like the shrouded dead on Resurrection Morn. 'God preserve us all,' she cried. 'Why ever not?'

'They failed to see eye to eye,' said Gaylord. He went and put his head round Auntie Rose's door. 'Did you say you *did* want tea?' he asked.

Auntie Rose jerked convulsively, fastened her eyes on her book, and did not reply.

'Poppa didn't sleep with Momma,' Gaylord said. The effect on Auntie Rose was remarkable. She held out her arms. 'Oh, you poor lamb,' she cried.

Gaylord wondered why he had suddenly become a poor lamb. But he remembered he had a duty to perform. He took a cup to Auntie Becky. 'Did Rose have one?' she asked.

'She didn't seem to want one,' Gaylord said.

Auntie Becky smiled. Gaylord carried a cup to Poppa. Poppa took one look and turned his face again to the wall. 'I told Grandpa and everybody you were in the attic,' Gaylord said, thoughtfully twisting one of the eyes of the stuffed owl.

'Dear child,' said Poppa.

'Is the tea all right?'

'Delicious. You're sure you didn't get the hemlock by mistake?'

'I don't *think so*,' said Gaylord, wondering vaguely which tin Momma kept the hemlock in. 'I'm going to get dressed now.'

'Do that,' said his father thankfully.

Like hibernators at the call of spring, the family began to stir into life. With a sigh Auntie Rose slipped a leather bookmark into her psychopathology, pulled a dressing gown over her sensible nightie, looked at herself in the mirror, shuddered, and set off down the corridor. She tried a door handle. Locked. She knocked irritably. 'Shan't be a minute,' Gaylord called cheerfully from within.

Auntie Becky pulled a frothy negligé over her frilly pyjamas, gave herself a congratulatory smile in the mirror, and set off down the corridor. Locked. She beat a tattoo on the door. 'Shan't be a minute,' Gaylord called cheerfully from within.

Next it was Momma. 'Gaylord, if you're going to stay in there all morning I shall make you use the outside loo.'

Gaylord sighed. He didn't like the outside loo. The hole was so big and deep he knew he'd fall in one day and get swept out to sea. 'Shan't be a minute,' he called.

Grandpa, scratching his chest, pulled on his long, yellowing pants, yawned. Sunday, he thought. And the whole blasted family under his feet. Rose and Becky stalking each other like a couple of cats. That fool Jocelyn refusing to sleep with a damned handsome woman like May. Gaylord! And the November cold seeping into the great house.

Grandpa was squat, broad-shouldered, and powerful, with the build of a rather stunted oak. He seldom smiled, never laughed, though often he would be seen shaking with deep-down private laughter that never quite broke surface. He had been in practice as a solicitor till he was sixty. Then he had retired, bought the farm he had longed for all his life, and was now trying to cram a lifetime of fulfilment into his few declining years. He was cantankerous, intolerant, prejudiced and intensely sentimental. Now he shaved, damning and blasting as the razor sliced into the grey stubblefield of his chin. He tied his tie in a thick knot, put on his jacket, and came down to breakfast.

They were all there, waiting. He grunted, and opened the *Observer*, ostentatiously chucking the review section on to the floor. He had never forgiven the paper for splitting itself into two, like a damned intellectual amoeba as he put it. But for the memory of the late J L Garvin, whom he revered, he'd have switched to the *Telegraph*.

Jocelyn, he was pleased to see, was looking sheepish. May was brittle and composed. Becky, as always, looked like a cat who has just been at the cream. Rose – Rose was one with the dank, damp, cheerless November day.

Gaylord, suddenly remembering that he was a poor lamb, burst into tears. 'What the devil's the matter with him?' demanded Grandpa.

'You may well ask,' Auntie Rose said darkly.

'Well, I am asking, dammit.'

Auntie Rose looked meaningly at Momma and Poppa. 'I think his parents could tell us,' she said.

Poppa shook a couple of aspirins out of his bottle, swallowed them, and looked sick.

Rose said, 'Even if you have no thought for each other, you might have some for the child.'

'My egg's bad,' said Gaylord, who had grown tired of being a poor lamb, and detested eggs.

'You have no idea what harm a shock like this morning's might have on his little mind,' said Auntie Rose.

'The only thing that could harm *his* little mind would be a Sherman tank,' said Grandpa. 'And even then I don't know which would come off worst.'

'My egg stinks like hell,' said Gaylord.

'Gaylord!' Momma said sharply.

'Freud clearly states – ' began Auntie Rose.

Grandpa banged the table. '*That* man!' he shouted.

'What man?' asked Auntie Rose.

'Frood,' said Grandpa.

'My egg's got a chicken inside,' said Gaylord.

Great Aunt Marigold put her oar in. 'Now, Rose. You know quite well your father forbids any mention of Frood at breakfast time.'

Rose drummed her fists on the table. 'If only you wouldn't call him *Frood*,' she cried hysterically.

'There you go again,' said Grandpa. He rose, flung down his napkin, and left the room. Great Aunt Marigold hurried after him crying. 'See what you've done, Rose. Now he will spend the entire day hiding his dudgeon behind the pages of the *Observer*.'

Momma looked at Rose. 'Now then,' she said briskly, 'What's on your mind?'

Rose looked anxiously at Gaylord. But he was busy screwing up one eye and squinting into his egg. She said, 'I'm talking about you making Jocelyn s-l-e-e-p in the a-t-t-i-c.'

'She didn't make me,' said Poppa. 'I took umbrage and went.'

'Nonsense, I threw you out and flung your slumberwear after you.'

Poppa rose. 'If even my slumberwear is to be dragged in – ' He shrugged and left the room.

'I can see its beak,' said Gaylord.

Chapter 2

Rose was a nice woman. She taught in the town at the Gas Works Lane Mixed Infants. She had no vocation for teaching. Though she liked a few individual children, collectively she found them revolting. They were, she thought, viciously cruel, dirty-minded, and dishonest. At thirty the acid of approaching spinsterhood was already beginning to corrode. And today she was more on edge than usual, for she knew that she was committed to pressing a switch that would turn the floodlight full on her. All through breakfast she had braved herself to make her announcement. But the Gaylord thing had snowballed, as things almost always did in the family. So now it had to be at lunch. She couldn't leave it later than that.

She swallowed, went red, and took the plunge. 'I shall be – '

'Quiet, damn you,' snarled Grandpa, who had just reached a tricky point in the carving, and required all his concentration.

Rose was silent. Oh, Lord, is it worth it? she thought.

Grandpa finished the hacking and the mutilation. Rose tried again. 'I shall be having a friend in to supper,' she announced.

Now, she thought. That's done it. There's no going back now.

But to her surprise there was no reaction. Becky said, without interest, 'Who is she? Do I know her?' To Becky, Rose's friends were indistinguishable. They were tweedy and arch; just, but only just, on the feminine side of neuter; they laughed a lot, without any real humour; they discussed art and literature with seriousness but without perception or understanding. Not that Becky cared a fig about art or literature. She just knew phonies when she saw them.

But this was the moment of truth. Rose said, 'It's a Mr Roberts. He teaches in the Senior School.'

'Rose!' Becky's eyes were alight with laughter and interest. 'A man!'

Great Aunt Marigold's hearing-aid was excellent. But she always liked to get confirmation of important news items. 'What does she say, John?' she asked.

'Says she's got a chap coming to supper,' bellowed Grandpa.

'My, my.' Aunt Marigold beamed and chortled. 'Rose, sweethearting at her age.'

'It's not like that,' Rose said hotly.

'Is he Auntie Rose's lover?' Gaylord asked, shovelling in his mess of gravy and mashed potato.

Rose's sallow face had flushed to an unpleasant, dull purple. 'Bobs – Mr Roberts – is just a friend. We – we have a common interest in psychology. That's all.' She floundered on. 'There's – nothing silly.'

'I don't call sex silly,' Becky said with conviction.

'Well, there's nothing like that, anyway,' said Rose.

Gaylord looked out of the window. 'It's getting *ever* so foggy,' he pointed out. 'I bet if Auntie Rose's lover does come he'll have to stay the night. He'll have to sleep with —'

'Gaylord!' cried Momma, not knowing what was coming, but fearing the worst.

'Sleep with Poppa in the attic,' went on Gaylord, refusing to be put off.

'I'm not sleeping in the attic,' said Poppa.

'Aren't you, dear?' Momma asked sweetly.

But Rose was looking anxiously out of the window. Gaylord had been right. The fog was moving in like a besieging army, rising up from the grey fields, billowing into the lanes. Suppose, after all this, Bobs didn't come. A fine fool she'd look. A fine song and dance the family would make about it. It wasn't fair. Nothing ever kept Becky's young men away. They came, swift and confident as eagles, sweeping in in their sports cars, thundering in on their powerful motorbikes. But Bobs, peering through the windscreen of his old Morris, Bobs was different. God, let him come, she prayed, thinking that if he didn't she would die of mortification and frustrated love.

'Getting thicker,' Gaylord announced cheerfully. 'I bet Auntie Rose's lover won't even get here.'

'Oh, shut up,' Auntie Rose said rudely.

Gaylord didn't approve of Sunday afternoons. Everybody went to sleep. He decided to do his disappearing act.

He slipped out into the stack yard. And the fog swallowed him up.

Gaylord loved fog. It would be quite easy, he decided, to get lost. All the family out searching for him with hurricane lamps, and at last finding his small body, cold and stiff, only half a mile from home. He nearly made himself cry.

The daylight was already fading. There were deep pools of darkness under the trees, which loomed up like giants waiting to pounce. Gaylord set off down the lane. In his heart he knew it was going to be difficult to get lost. But there was no harm in trying.

13

He came to a favourite place, an old quarry overhung with trees, its floor a tangle of silver birch and the dead stalks of rosebay willow herb, and brambles to which a few seedy blackberries still hung. The fog was thickest here. The silence intense. Gaylord tramped in through the undergrowth.

'Hello, Gaylord,' said a sweet, gentle voice.

Gaylord was frightened out of his life. But he didn't show it. He stood still.

'What you doing?' said the voice.

Gaylord peered. He saw a pale moon face smiling a welcome through the fog. 'I knew it was you, all the time, Willie,' he said, immensely relieved.

'It's foggy,' said Willie. 'You coming a walk?'

This was exciting. In addition to the possibility of getting lost, there was the fact that Momma had forbidden him to talk to Willie, Willie being only ninepence to the shilling. Gaylord didn't know anyone else who was only ninepence to the shilling, so it was just like Momma to stop him meeting anyone with such a fascinating trait.

Willie put out a large hand and took Gaylord's. They set off.

'Quiet, isn't it,' said Willie.

It was indeed. Not a sound from bird or beast or man. Once a yellow pane of light glowed softly in the dusk, and was left behind. Silence, fog, the damp roadway, the wet, yellowing grass at its verge. Nothing else in the whole wide world.

They walked on. And the stratum of sound common sense that was never very far below the surface of Gaylord's mind rose to the top. 'Do you think we're lost, Willie?' he asked, slowing down.

'Yes,' said Willie, his grip tightening.

Gaylord dug in his toes. 'I'm going back now,' he said.

Willie tugged. 'You're scared,' he said.

'No, I'm not,' said Gaylord.

They had a tug of war in the silent lane. But Willie was eighteen, and his body was stronger than his poor weak mind. Gaylord could not escape. 'Got something to show you,' Willie said, cajoling.

'What?'

'Wait till you see,' said Willie.

Perhaps Willie had found buried treasure. Grudgingly Gaylord went a little further. But now the fog seemed to be impregnated with sound. It grew louder. The fog in front grew luminous, concentrated itself into two mistily-bright yellow eyes. The car stopped with a jerk. 'Gaylord,' called a voice.

'Ta-ra,' said Willie, fading into the fog.

Gaylord went and peered into the small red sports car. He was disappointed to find it wasn't a search party. It was one of Auntie Becky's young men. 'Would you like to get in and show me the way, Gaylord?' he asked politely.

'If you like,' Gaylord said generously. He climbed in. Five minutes later he had merged unobtrusively into the life of the household.

Or so he thought. But Momma suddenly looked at him sharply and said, 'Where have you been?'

'Out,' Gaylord said meekly.

'Out where?'

'Just out,' said Gaylord. With devilish cunning he changed the subject. 'Has Auntie Rose's lover come yet?'

To his relief he had succeeded. Auntie Rose snapped, 'Mr Roberts isn't coming till supper time,' and Red Sports Car, happily holding hands with Becky on the settee, pricked up his ears and said, 'What's this, Roe? Have you got hidden depths?'

'I bet he won't come,' said Gaylord. 'I bet you anything he won't come.'

'All right,' Auntie Rose said in a tightly controlled voice. 'He won't come.'

'It's getting thicker and thicker and thicker,' said Gaylord. 'I bet if he tries to come he'll have an accident.'

Auntie Rose said, a little wildly, 'Perhaps even now he's lying in a pool of gore.'

Gaylord considered this. 'What's gore?' he asked.

'Blood. Thick, sticky blood.'

'Gore,' said Gaylord. 'Gore, gore, gore, gore.' It was a good word. He liked it. He stored it for future use. He thought of something else. 'I bet Auntie Becky's young man will have to stay the night, too. He'll have to sleep – '

Grandpa flung down the *Observer*. 'Will you stop deciding who sleeps with who in this house.'

Gaylord was hurt. 'I only said – '

'Well, don't.'

Gaylord addressed himself to Auntie Becky's young man. 'Poppa slept in the attic,' he said conversationally. 'He and Momma failed to see eye to eye about money.'

Darkness and fog crept and crawled and deepened about the house. But inside the fire danced, and the family settled down for Sunday evening. Becky and her young man held hands and giggled occasionally. Rose sat with Freud open on her lap, pretending to read when she thought anyone was watching her, gazing into space when they weren't. Grandpa was still working his way through the vast open spaces of the *Observer*. Momma was making a stair carpet. Great Aunt Marigold, Poppa and Gaylord passed the time in meditation.

Aunt Marigold's old mind was like a time machine with erratic steering, transporting her from the present to the distant past: from old, unhappy far-off things to tomorrow's dinner. The trouble was that nowadays she was becoming confused as to which was which. Sometimes Victoria was still on the throne, sometimes Elizabeth. Sometimes the friends of her youth, who had one by one stolen silently into the shadows, were still with her, more real than her present companions. Sometimes Gaylord was Gaylord; at other times he was the Poppa of thirty years ago, when the world was young and sweet, and summer's lease had longer dates than these present, cheerless intervals between spring and autumn.

Poppa meditated, pen in hand, virgin sheet before him. Like most humorous writers, he was of a melancholic and haunted disposition. Like most humorous writers, he would have liked to have written *Hamlet* if the Bard hadn't nipped in first, a fact that filled him with a certain resentment against the top brass of English lit. His unconscious mind was bubbling with conflicts and tragic irony. But he had to be funny. It was all he could be. 'Laugh, clown, laugh,' he muttered grimly, and began to write.

Gaylord's little mind was seething happily. First there was the question of Willie's buried treasure. There was room for endless speculation here. At the first possible moment he intended to seek out Willie, whatever Momma might say. There was the intriguing thought of Auntie Rose's lover. There was the question of what Auntie Becky and her young man could see in holding hands. Lastly, there was the impending battle of bedtime. Any time at all now, if he knew Momma, she was going to say, 'Bed, Gaylord,' and he'd got to be ready with a counter-offensive. He went to the window, pulled aside the curtain, and pressed his nose against the cold glass. 'It's getting worse and worse,' he said.

'Bed, Gaylord,' said Momma.

He turned, affronted. 'It isn't six o'clock, yet,' he cried in incredulous astonishment.

'It will be in a minute,' said Momma.

'The clock's fast,' said Gaylord.

'Come on. Clear those things up.'

That was another thing about Momma. She rode roughshod over logical argument. 'Grandpa said it was fast,' complained Gaylord.

'That was a week ago,' said Grandpa.

Gaylord thought quickly. 'Well, if it was fast a week ago it must be even faster, now.'

'I put it right,' said Grandpa.

No support. Gaylord tried another tack. 'I shouldn't think Auntie Rose's lover will come now,' he said.

'Bed,' said Momma.

Gaylord delivered himself of a considered judgement. 'I should think he either won't come; or he's had an accident.'

'Or both,' muttered Poppa from the writing table.

Gaylord brightened. This was a pot that it might be possible to keep boiling. 'Yes. If he'd had an accident he wouldn't come because he'd be in hospital, covered in – gore.'

'Or dead,' said Poppa.

'I'll give you till I've counted ten,' said Momma. 'One, two –'

'Can't I stay and see Auntie Rose's lover?'

'Three. Four. You've just said he won't come.'

'*But he might*, Momma.'

'Thanks,' Auntie Rose said bitterly.

'Five. Six. We're nearly there, Gaylord.'

Gaylord thought desperately. He looked at Auntie Becky and her young man. 'Why don't you and Poppa hold hands?' he asked.

'Ten,' said Momma. 'Bed.'

Gaylord knew when he was beaten. 'Good night, all,' he said briskly capitulating. He kissed Auntie Rose unenthusiastically, Becky pleasurably, Momma and Poppa perfunctorily, and Grandpa passionately, this last not so much from affection as because he liked the scratchy feel of Grandpa's cheek.

As the door closed behind him there were sighs of relief; the long evening settled about them as the fire settled in the hearth.

Auntie Rose thought: I'll give him till half past six. Then if he's not come, I'll put him right out of my mind.

At half past six she thought: he could still come. He could have taken a wrong turn in the fog and been delayed. At seven she looked at Becky and thought: why has she always got a young man on hand? Nothing ever stops *them* coming. But the first time I ask a man to supper he has to be prevented by fog. And I am thirty, and time is growing desperately short.

At eight she longed for the evening to pass. Normally she clung to this weekend break from the hours of teaching. But all she wanted now was to get back to the Mixed Infants and the possibility of seeing dear Bobs.

Suppertime came. They went in. To her relief nobody mentioned the vacant chair. Eventually she was able to go up to her room. She looked out. The fog lay against the window like a dirty grey army blanket. The world outside was empty of life. Today had been empty, the past and the future were empty. If Bobs loved her, really loved her, he would have come, though it were ten thousand mile. But now she knew the truth.

Chapter 3

The fog, having done its dirty work, folded its tents like the Arab and stole away during the night. Monday morning was bright and gay, as though the calendar had suddenly slipped back to September. In the stack yard a bird sang, one last joyous outburst before the silence of winter. Gaylord, waking, hurried off to see Momma and Poppa. But they had forestalled him. They were together, up and dressed already. They smiled at him blandly. 'Thirsting for information?' asked Poppa.

Gaylord felt rather hurt. They weren't taking him into their confidence. 'Did Poppa sleep in the attic?' he asked.

They smiled at him again. Then at each other. They said nothing. Gaylord drifted away. He was losing interest. He spent a meditative half hour locked in the loo. Then he went to the village school, where he absorbed learning with the detached efficiency of a sponge soaking up water.

Auntie Becky was picked up in a green sports car, and whisked off into town, where she performed with charm and surprising competence the job of private secretary.

Auntie Rose pedalled furiously, on an old sit-up-and-beg bicycle, the two miles to the station. She was going to see Bobs. She perched impatiently on the edge of a seat in a cold second-class compartment, while the train chugged importantly through the bright morning. Soon it was pulling into the station. Perhaps, she thought, perhaps Bobs will be on the platform to meet me. He never had been. But today was different. There were explanations, apologies, forgivings that might not be possible in the staff common room. She put her head out of the window. The platform was empty. She hurried to school. The train had been late, and by the time she arrived the staff were in their classrooms, beginning another week's fight to fill uncaring or hostile minds with the best that has been thought or written. She did not see Bobs until the morning break.

He was on the far side of the staff room, caught up with that bore Symons. He saw her, and looked away. But at last he was working his way across the crowded room. 'Wasn't it a stinker,' he said. 'You didn't expect me, of course.'

'Good heavens, no,' she said.

'You don't get J R Roberts out in that weather,' he said. 'Got too much respect for his own skin.'

'It would have been awfully foolish.'

'Foolish! You can say that again.' He smiled confidently down at her. 'I wouldn't have gone out last night for the Queen of England.'

'Perhaps you'd like to come next week, instead,' she suggested, playing anxiously with a propelling pencil.

'OK,' he said. 'If you can guarantee better weather.'

'I'll do my best,' she said lightly, with a breaking heart. She lowered her voice. 'I was disappointed you couldn't come, Bobs.'

'Yes, but I mean to say, can't help the English climate, can we?'

The bell rang. She gave him a wan smile. 'I'll have to get back to my kids.'

'That's right,' he said. 'Back to the old treadmill.' He knocked out his pipe.

Still she could not tear herself away. 'Next Sunday, then,' she said. 'All being well.'

'All being well,' he said absently, sorting out his books. He went, and she knew she had gone straight out of his mind.

'Come straight home,' Momma had said; and Gaylord did, nearly. He just made a slight *détour* into the old quarry.

The bright morning had not kept up its promise. About midday a high, filmy cloud had appeared near the sun and had slowly descended, first diluting and then blotting out the sunshine, and spreading a cold chill over the dank earth. And the invisible sun went down towards its setting, and by the time Gaylord reached the quarry the dusk was lying heavy on the land. Gaylord tramped into the wet undergrowth. And there was Willie, doing nothing as effortlessly as a tree.

'What were you going to show me?' asked Gaylord.

'You wouldn't come,' said Willie.

'I will now.'

Willie stirred sluggishly. 'Come on, then,' he said.

They set off along the damp lanes.

They were going towards the river. They left the lane and turned down a path between high hedges of box; a path littered and strewn with dying nettles and dock. They came into the water meadows.

In this last moment of the day the cloud had thinned, and bars of feeble, watery light lay across the swirl of the river, and touched the crumbling stones of an old fishermen's hut. Willie led the way to the hut. Once again a warning bell rang in Gaylord's brain. 'Where are we going?' he asked, slowly.

'It's in there,' said Willie.

Gaylord ignored the warning bell. This was just the place for buried treasure. They went into the tumbledown hut. Its stone floor was riven by thrusting trees and bushes, its roof fallen in these many years. There was a hearth, with a blackened, broken grate. Willie looked at Gaylord with sudden suspicion, almost hostility. He grabbed his arm. 'Promise you won't tell,' he said.

'Promise,' said Gaylord, performing an elaborate secrecy rite that included crossing himself, spitting, and going cross-eyed.

Willie went to the grate. He pulled off a cover of dried grass. Gaylord went and peered, awestruck. There, lying in its nest of stalk and leaf, was the most beautiful thing Gaylord had ever seen. Even in this dying light it glowed and shone. Reverently Willie lifted it out. Gaylord peered, agog. 'What is it?'

'A paperweight,' said Willie.

'What's it for?'

'Dunno.' Willie was running his fat, white fingers lovingly over the smooth glass, gazing with love and affection at the picture that was caught forever like a fly in amber, of Leeds Town Hall. 'Let me hold it,' said Gaylord.

Very carefully Willie handed it over to him. It was terribly heavy, a large, smooth circle of glass in which was enshrined the pretty picture. It was lovely to touch, beautiful to look at. Gaylord was fascinated. But suddenly Willie snatched it from him, roughly but carefully. He put it back, covered it as reverently as a priest the sacred vessels, looked round at Gaylord with his mixture of suspicion and hostility. 'Bet you'll go and tell someone.'

'Shan't,' said Gaylord. He repeated his ritual.

'I wish I hadn't shown it you,' said Willie. Suddenly his pale, flabby features crumpled into tears. 'You'll tell someone and they'll take it away,' he snivelled.

'I shan't, Willie,' said Gaylord.

Willie put up a hand and dashed away his tears. He looked cunning. 'I shall kill you if you do,' he said with simple conviction.

Gaylord shivered deliciously. But he stuck his hands in his trouser pockets to give an air of casualness as he asked, 'Have you ever killed anyone, Willie?'

Willie opened his mouth to reply. Then the look of half-witted cunning came back. 'Come on,' he said, and roughly he dragged Gaylord out of the hut, and away to where the lights of the village were already yellow in the gloom.

Gaylord came home, hands in pockets, blowing air through his front teeth in what he imagined was a careless whistle. Momma took one look at him and said, 'Hullo! What have you been up to?'

'Nothing,' said Gaylord, looking and sounding and feeling hurt.

'It's taken you a long time.'

'What has?'

'Doing nothing.'

'I've been to *school*,' Gaylord said.

'I mean since then.'

Gaylord looked puzzled. 'I've been coming home.'

'You must be a very slow walker.'

He limped agonizingly across the kitchen. 'Hurt my leg,' he said. 'Teacher thinks it may be broken.'

She was looking at him in a way he didn't like. 'Have you been talking to Willie?' she asked accusingly.

Momma had a terribly suspicious mind. Gaylord never ceased to be shocked by what he felt was a very serious defect of character. He looked at her with blue-eyed, pained innocence. But it was a strange thing about Gaylord. Devious-mindedness and equivocation were meat and drink to him; but when it came to a downright, thumping lie his mind set up a block. 'Well, not exactly talking,' he said.

'Exactly what, then?' asked Momma, looking about seven feet high. But now Gaylord had got them successfully off the straight up-and-down lines of truth and falsehood, on to the rambling branch line of suggestion and prevarication. 'He just said, "Good evening, Gaylord," and I said, "Good evening, Willie." ' He began to sound indignant again. 'I couldn't not say, "Good evening, Willie," could I, when he said, "Good evening, Gaylord"?'

'Then what?' asked Momma.

'Then I came home,' said Gaylord. After all, he had. Here he was to prove it.

'Straight home?' asked Momma.

Some people could never take a statement at its face value. 'Almost,' said Gaylord, thinking he had now opened the floodgates to a full cross-examination.

But to his surprise Momma didn't follow it up. She sat down, put her hands on his shoulders, looked at him very gravely and said, 'Gaylord, you are not to talk to Willie, or see him. I mean it.'

'But why, Momma?'

There was a silence. Then: 'I don't know, Gaylord, I really don't know,' Momma said, almost as though she were talking to a grown-up. 'I just feel it's – unwise.'

'Because he's only ninepence to the shilling?'

'That's a very unkind thing to say,' said Momma. 'But – yes, I suppose that's why.'

Momma was looking very thoughtful. Gaylord decided the time was ripe to attempt a tactical disengagement. 'Did Auntie Rose's lover come?' he asked.

'I want you to promise,' said Momma.

'Promise what?' asked Gaylord, as if he didn't know.

'Not to see Willie.'

He performed his secrecy ritual. 'Gaylord,' Momma cried, scandalized. 'Don't let me ever see you do that again.'

'Sorry, Momma,' Gaylord said contritely, realizing he hadn't actually promised and anxious now to stop Momma realizing it too. 'Teacher says if you go cock-eyed when the wind's in the east you'll stay like it.'

'You're not to say "cock-eyed",' said Momma.

They were heading away from Willie, out into the open water. 'Teacher says "cock-eyed",' said Gaylord.

Momma sighed. If teacher said half the things Gaylord reported her as saying, she must have a very odd mind. 'Can we have tea, soon?' Gaylord asked, putting a few more miles between themselves and Willie.

'He's been seeing Willie again,' said Momma. 'But I've made him promise not to.'

'Did you get it in writing?' asked Poppa.

'I think you can trust him, if he's promised.'

'*If* he's promised. Are you sure he did, without any reservations, mental or otherwise?'

Momma considered. 'I think so. But how can I or anyone else know what's going on in that tortuous little mind?'

It was, indeed, a very good question. Poppa said, 'Willie's probably perfectly harmless, anyway.'

'I wonder,' said Momma. 'He's got a charming smile, I must say, and he seems so gentle. But he makes my flesh creep. I can imagine him doing almost anything.'

Friday evening, and another week of boredom and irritation over. Rose came upon Bobs just as he was getting his bicycle out of the shed. Did he really look, for a moment, trapped?

She was past caring. 'Shall we be seeing you on Sunday?' she asked.

'Oh. Ah. Yes. As a matter of fact I'm not *quite* sure – '

'Do try,' she said. She knew she shouldn't. The more you chased them the harder they ran. But if you didn't – you'd lost them anyway. It was a vicious circle; a problem that girls like Rose never solved, a problem that, for girls like Becky, didn't even exist.

He was younger than Rose. He had sleek black hair, and a neat little black moustache. His suit was a little too tight, his tie a little too vivid, his shoes a little too long, his smile far too quickly on and off. Assorted pens and ballpoints stuck up out of his breast pocket like broken teeth. Meeting him, most men would have found him wanting. But Rose felt herself melting for love of him. 'Try to come,' she said again.

'OK,' he said, rather grumpily. 'I'll do my best. About eight?'

She had been going to say six. 'Make it a bit earlier if you can,' she said.

'Right. Quarter to.' He gave her his quick perfunctory smile and jumped into the saddle. He'll come. Rose thought, but without joy. She felt humiliated, she didn't know why. It wasn't Bob's fault, of course. It was her own, for lowering herself like that. But she'd had to, hadn't she. Otherwise he would not be coming, and the world would be as empty as before.

But this Sunday Rose made no announcement. She couldn't face it. It would be soon enough when Bobs came – if he came. She waited in a nervous agony, as alert as a dog on the hearth. At seven o'clock she heard something. A car was coming up the lane, up the drive. It stopped. Rose half stood up, her hands fluttering about her throat. But Becky said in a matter of fact tone, 'Sounds like Peter,' and ran to the door.

It was Peter. They came in, laughing and holding hands. Rose could have killed them both.

Her nervous tension increased almost to breaking point. Supper was at seven-thirty. But because she had been too weak to tell Bobs this, she was faced with the dreadful alternatives of either asking for supper to be delayed and explaining why, or of having Bobs arrive in the middle of the meal, with all the confusion that this would involve.

Seven twenty-five. And no Bobs. But Grandpa was raucously asleep under the *Observer*, and so long as Grandpa slept there would be no supper. Don't let him wake, she prayed, sitting as quiet as a mouse. Then, on the stroke of seven-thirty, Grandpa surfaced from under the paper, looked balefully round, and said, 'Well, are we having anything to eat tonight, or aren't we?'

Rose said bravely, 'Could we wait just a few minutes? Mr Roberts may be coming.'

'Who?' barked Grandpa.

'Mr Roberts. He was coming last week, if you remember, but – '

'But he didn't. Doesn't look as though he's coming this week, either.' Grandpa struggled to his feet.

'He said he might not be able to come until later,' said the unhappy Rose.

Grandpa sat down again, trunk-like legs apart. He scowled at his watch. 'Give him five minutes,' he said.

Five minutes passed. Grandpa snapped shut his hunter, rose, and made for the dining-room. 'I am not having my entire household disorganized by a mythical Mr Roberts,' he said. 'We are having supper.'

And have supper they did. And they were well into the cold beef and pickles before a cheerful, confident knock sounded on the front door.

Rose leapt up as though she had been shot. 'Steady, girl, steady,' cried Becky, enjoying every moment. 'Don't rush your fences.'

Rose moderated her speed from six to two mph. She went and opened the door. 'Hello, Bobs,' she said shyly. 'I'm afraid we've had to start supper.'

He said, rather stuffily, 'I didn't think I was late.'

'You're not,' she said hurriedly. 'It's just that Father –' She trailed off. 'Let me take your coat.'

He let himself be led, blinking, into the dining room. 'This is Bobs,' she said.

'Is this your sweetheart, Rose?' Aunt Marigold asked, beaming happily.

'I wouldn't say that,' bawled Mr Roberts, who always assumed that anyone over sixty-five was both deaf and witless.

'And that's May. And Jocelyn my brother. My sister Becky.' Becky smiled fetchingly. 'Peter. And this is my father.'

Grandpa rose courteously, bowed, and sat down again. But in doing so he managed to make it quite clear that he hated the guts of anyone who interrupted his beef and pickles. He went on eating, casting occasional sidelong, suspicious glances at the newcomer as though fearing he would filch the food from under his very nose. But courtesy prevailed. 'Better pull a chair up,' he said between mouthfuls.

This was helpful so far as it went. The only trouble was that there wasn't a chair, and if there had been there wasn't room to pull it up, the family presenting a tight phalanx round the table.

Rose, who was agitated beyond all coherent thought and action, fussed about ineffectually. 'Budge up, you lot,' ordered Grandpa, whereupon they all put their hands under the sides of their chairs and, half rising, jerked themselves to left or right as the fancy took them. Now things were taking shape. A space had been made, next to Becky of course. Great Aunt Marigold had produced a plate. Grandpa was impatiently carving, and Rose, gathering her wits, fetched a chair from the kitchen. Bobs sat down. 'Pickles?' said Becky, with the air of a beautiful Circassian slave girl offering sweetmeats to the Sultan.

'Ta,' said Bobs, looking hungrily at his plate of beef. If someone would only give him a knife and fork he could start. But the family seemed to have exhausted their efforts. Rose was sitting gazing at him. The rest were tucking in vigorously, anxious to make up for lost time. Bobs made appealing pantomime gestures to Rose. She smiled fondly. 'Could I – ?' began Bobs. But at that moment the door opened. Gaylord, his pyjama legs in their usual position at half mast, stood framed in the doorway. He was smiling sweetly. 'Gaylord!' cried Momma. 'Why aren't you in bed?'

'I've come to see Auntie Rose's lover,' said Gaylord.

'Oh, Lord,' said Bobs. Sweetheart had been bad enough. He began to wonder what they thought his position in this household was. Even a shotgun wedding seemed a possibility when you looked at the old chap.

'You should have been asleep long ago,' said Momma.

'I was,' said Gaylord reasonably. 'But I woke up.'

'Well, say hello to Mr Roberts. Then back you go.'

'Hello,' Gaylord said without much interest. He didn't quite know what he'd expected. But he was definitely disappointed. Mr Roberts looked as ordinary as anybody else.

'Hello,' said Bobs, with an equal lack of interest. He was filled with misgivings. This girl Rose seemed to have been giving her family a brightly coloured version of their relationship. He'd have to be careful, he decided. Very, very careful. And he *still* hadn't a knife and fork.

Gaylord went round and kissed everybody, just to pass the time. 'Mr Roberts hasn't eaten his beef,' he said. 'Don't you like it?' Grandpa asked belligerently.

'I haven't a knife and fork,' Mr Roberts said, almost equally belligerently.

'Good God,' said Grandpa. Sitting there, not saying a word! How wet could you get? 'Give him some eating irons, someone,' he ordered.

'I'm *so* sorry, Bobs.' Rose was almost in tears. She produced a knife and fork. 'Ta,' said Bobs, injecting a world of irony into the disgusting monosyllable.

'Off you go, Gaylord,' said Momma. What a one-track mind the woman had.

'I'm hungry,' said Gaylord.

'You may have one biscuit.'

'Ta,' said Gaylord.

'What did you say?' Poppa asked menacingly. He would have been prepared to overlook little things like lying or theft, but when it came to debasing the mother tongue he put on what Momma called his Barrett of Wimpole Street act. 'What did you say?'

'Ta,' said Gaylord, confident in the fact that he could see at least two moves ahead.

'How many times – ?' began Poppa, exasperated.

31

'Mr Roberts said "Ta",' Gaylord pointed out. Had he been old enough to know about chess he would have added 'Check'.

'When you are as old as Mr Roberts – ' Poppa began the stock reply. Gaylord wasn't impressed. But Momma, riding roughshod as always over the cut and thrust of dialectic argument, got hold of Gaylord and bundled him out of the room. When she returned Grandpa looked at her admiringly. 'Always prefer *fortiter in re* to *suaviter in modo* meself, what do you say, Mr Robinson?'

'Roberts,' said Bobs. 'Pardon?'

Grandpa scowled. And went on with his meal. He wasn't going to waste his time explaining things in words of two syllables.

Becky turned to Bobs. She smiled, radiantly, giving him a momentary feeling of vertigo. 'Father means he's a great believer in a clip over the ear.'

'Oh,' said Bobs. 'Thank you very much.' He smiled back.

'Always glad to be of service,' Becky said with another brilliant smile. For a second a firm, soft knee touched his. He had again that sensation of falling. He looked up and found Rose's eyes fixed longingly on him from the far side of the table. 'Have you got all you need, Bobs?' she asked.

'Yes, ta,' said Bobs.

Rose racked her brains, and couldn't think of another thing to say. Damn Becky, she was thinking. She's got one man and now she's after mine. Just for the hell of it. But Becky could no more help reacting to men than petrol could help reacting to a lighted match. 'What do you do, Mr Roberts?' she cooed.

'I teach,' said Bobs.

'Oh, for God's sake,' said Grandpa.

'Pardon?' said Bobs, looking alarmed.

Couldn't the damn feller say anything but 'pardon'? Becky, acting again as interpreter, said, 'Father doesn't believe in teachers.'

Mr Roberts pondered this remarkable statement. Rose said, 'Don't take any notice of him, Bobs. *I* think teaching is a noble profession.'

'Oh, so do I,' said Becky with deep conviction.

'Damn long holidays, anyway,' said Peter, uttering for the first time. He laughed nervously.

Grandpa gave him a sour look. 'Have to have,' he said. 'How else do you think they'd get anyone to do the job?'

Bobs said stiffly, 'There's such a thing as a vocation, sir.'

'Not in teaching,' Grandpa said firmly.

Becky said, 'Father, you're being very unkind and unfair to Mr Roberts.'

'Me?' Grandpa looked incredulous.

'Your manners are a bloody disgrace,' Poppa said, still smarting under *suaviter in modo.*

Grandpa was genuinely appalled. If there was one thing he prided himself on it was his old world courtesy. He turned to Mr Roberts. 'My dear Mr Robertson. I do beg you to forgive me if I've said anything – I can only apologize, and ask you to put it down to the foolishness of age.'

'That's all right,' said Bobs. 'Some teachers are stinkers, anyway.'

'Do help yourself to, cheese,' said Grandpa. 'I can recommend the Stilton.'

At last the meal came to an end. They retired to the drawing-room. Rose, seeing Becky and Peter holding hands on the settee, thought: At last. Now I can get him to myself, away from that little so-and-so. 'Come and sit here, Bobs,' she said happily patting the chair next to her own.

But she had reckoned without Grandpa's conscience. 'Now, Mr Robertson. Come and talk to an old man. Tell me about the Burnham Scale,' said Grandpa, drawing up a chair next to his own.

'Thank you,' said Bobs, flattered.

Grandpa gave him a cigar. The evening passed. Grandpa and Mr Roberts got on like a house on fire. Becky smiled fondly at Peter; and, whenever she could catch his eye, which was pretty often, at Bobs. Rose had to content herself with the sight of her beloved, and the murmur of his voice. Aunt Marigold's mind was running a shuttle service between now and the 'nineties. Momma was worrying about Willie; why, she could not have said. It was just an undefinable sense of danger. Poppa had retired to that world of the imagination where he was undisputed King; more, where he was God; Creator, Disposer, Destroyer.

But even Grandpa's conscience went off duty at ten-thirty. He snapped open his hunter, yawned. 'Getting damn late,' he said.

The subtle hint was taken. Becky and Peter rose, slipped out of the room. Mr Roberts said, 'Well, time I was making tracks. Mustn't miss my beauty sleep at any cost.'

'You must come again,' Grandpa said. 'Enjoyed our chat enormously.'

'Ta,' said Bobs. He rose. 'Good night, all.'

'I'll come and get your coat,' said Rose. She was trembling violently. Now was the testing moment when the whole wretched evening might be redeemed. She would go out with him to the car, alone in the darkness. And there, under the stars, away from the family, away from the staff room, who could say what might happen? The pressure of fingers, a kiss, even his arms about her yielding body? They went into the hall. She helped him into his coat. 'Ta,' he said. 'See you at the old sweatshop, then.'

'I'll come with you to the car,' she said hurriedly.

They went out into the big, dark storm porch. 'Raining like hell,' he said.

Blast, she thought. 'We shall have to say goodbye here, then,' she said, her voice tight and uneven. She looked up at him in the darkness. She moved towards him. She could feel the rough tweed of his coat, the warmth of his being. 'Goodbye, Bobs,' she whispered with infinite tenderness.

'Don't make a meal of it, you two,' said a cheerful voice at her elbow. Rose jumped convulsively. 'Becky!' she said, her voice harsh with disappointment and at this moment, hate. 'What are you doing here?'

'Snogging, for want of a more elegant word,' Becky said happily.

In the darkness Rose could just make out two faces, very close together. 'Well, so long,' Bobs said cheerfully. And, with more interest, 'Good night, Becky.'

'Be seeing you,' said Becky.

Rose said wildly, 'I'll come to the car.'

'But you'll be soaked.'

'I'm coming,' she said.

But the mood, if there had ever been one, was shattered. Rose stood miserably in the downpour while Bobs leapt into the car, switched on the lights, started the engine, and drove off with a 'So long' and a wave. She came back into the porch. 'Parting is such sweet sorrow,' said Becky.

'Damn you,' Rose said viciously, and swept into the house. 'Is it raining?' asked Aunt Marigold, surprised.

'Like hell,' said Rose, and ran up to her room, where the tears burst from her like a summer storm.

'It's nice to see Rose sweethearting,' Great Aunt Marigold said. 'I do like to see young people happy.'

To her delight he came up to her in the staff room the following morning. He was smiling. 'Why didn't you tell me?' he asked in the friendliest of voices.

'Tell you what, Bobs?'

'That you'd got such a smasher for a sister.'

'Oh, Becky. Yes, she's very pretty, isn't she.'

'I'll say. The old gentleman's friendly, too. Funny thing, I was all ready to tell him where he got off at first.'

Rose said quietly, 'I'm afraid I didn't see much of you, Bobs.'

'That's all right,' he said absently, watching little Miss Jones bend down to pick up a book.

'You must come again,' she said, fighting to keep the un-happiness out of her voice.

'Yes, rather,' he said, with more enthusiasm than she could have hoped for. But how much of the enthusiasm was due to herself, and how much to Becky? This, she thought wretchedly, was a question she would perhaps never answer.

Chapter 4

November, month of the dead, All Saints, All Souls; mist drifting about the fields like the unquiet dead; the river running full, starred with yellow leaves, seeping in boggy pools into the water meadows, the beeches flaming one day bright as bonfires, the next standing still and dead and dank; the stack yard mired and brown-puddled; the spinneys mournfully dripping leaves and raindrops; the air soft, damp, and sweet in the pinewoods; the early dusk cloaking the hills; Wellingtons and plastic macs cluttering the porch.

Gaylord, gumbooted, plodded through every puddle he could find. At first, in his wanderings, he would see from a distance the old fishermen's hut where Willie's treasure lay. But as time went on he circled ever nearer to it. It drew him like a magnet. He could, of course, just go in and have a peep. But no. It was Willie's place. He couldn't go in without Willie.

Then, one day, he found himself, quite without his volition, on the very threshold. He didn't even know how he'd got there.

The wide landscape was empty. He went inside.

The hut was as it had been that other day. Gaylord's eyes were on the grate. The nest of leaves and grass was still there.

It couldn't hurt just to have a look. He lifted off the grassy covering, and gazed in delight. It was even more beautiful than he remembered. Leeds Town Hall shone with a light that never was on land or sea. With as much care as if he were handling the Crown Jewels he lifted it out. Touching it, holding it, gazing into its clear, limpid depths, he was filled with that wonder that only the child, the poet, and perhaps the idiot can ever know. He stayed, fondling his treasure, disregarding that old tyrant Time as only a child can. The thought of having it in his room, to play with at bedtime, and when he awoke, filled his mind. Willie would never know who had taken it. And anyway, Willie couldn't do anything. He was only ninepence to the shilling.

For the first time in his life Gaylord wrestled terribly with temptation. And won. He did not know why. But some deep, built-in sense of right and wrong came to his rescue. He put the precious, lovely thing back in its nest and went home, with a sense of loneliness and loss.

The winter crept on. Throughout the towns and cities of England elderly gentlemen (sober, must be fond of children) were putting on white whiskers and red habits and taking up position in the big stores. Christmas card manufacturers offered the Adoration of the Shepherds as an intellectual status symbol, robins on logs to elderly aunts, and damn great tinselled horrors to the pink-gin-old-boy belt. And so many charities were selling their own cards that it seemed likely that very soon a new charity would have to be formed. The Society for the Relief of Unemployed Commercial Christmas Card Manufacturers. Hideous and revolting novelties appeared on the counters of normally sensible shops like an angry rash. Everything from a suitcase to a kettle became a Yuletide Gift. In little backstreets the windows of dingy shops were festooned with blobs of cotton wool on string. Turkeys and geese and chickens hung in hundreds in the poulterers, proud, plump, and clean in sacrificial death. Christian England was preparing, once again, to make a few million in celebration of the birth of a Child to a peasant girl in the stable of an inn.

Momma had done the easy part of the Christmas Card operation. That is to say, she had bought fifty cards, and addressed, stamped, and posted forty-seven of them. The difficult part lay ahead: to cajole or bully Poppa into doing his three, one to an elderly aunt, the others to two old buddies from the RAF whom Poppa resolutely refused to forget, but equally resolutely refused to do anything about. Poppa would rather write a short story than address Christmas cards. He said they weren't creative.

The puddings were made. The whole family was treating Abdullah the turkey with a shamefaced cossetting the creature accepted with detached scorn. Poppa said to Momma, 'What do you think Gaylord would like for Christmas?'

Momma looked at Poppa in some surprise. For Poppa to take the initiative in anything to do with Christmas was quite unprecedented. 'What is on your little mind?' she asked.

'An electric train set,' said Poppa.

'I'll ask him,' said Momma. 'But you know Gaylord. He'll probably want something quite *outré*.'

Poppa looked sad. He said, 'My own train set consisted of a tiny clockwork engine that hurtled round the track so fast that it never accomplished more than one revolution. Then it would fly off and lie on its back, kicking and struggling like an upturned beetle.'

'Poor Jocelyn,' said Momma.

'So when I grew up I decided to marry and have children, in the hope that one would be a boy for whom I could buy an electric train set.'

'I always wondered,' said Momma. 'You never seemed the marrying type.'

'It was a long-term project. But now the time is ripe.'

'Don't set your heart on it too much,' said Momma. 'You're reckoning without Gaylord.'

As indeed she found when she interviewed the child. 'What would you like Father Christmas to bring you?' she asked.

'A paperweight,' Gaylord said without hesitation.

There was a silence. 'A what?' asked Momma.

'A paperweight.'

Momma's voice was controlled. 'What sort of a paperweight?'

'Just a paperweight,' said Gaylord.

'Poppa thought you might like an electric train set.'

Gaylord considered. 'I'd rather have a paperweight,' he said at last.

She came back to Poppa. 'You remember I said Gaylord might want something *outré*?'

Poppa looked forlorn. 'Go on,' he said.

'Guess how *outré*,' said Momma.

Poppa thought. He shook his head. 'Imagination boggles,' he admitted.

'A paperweight,' said Momma.

The silence was heavy. 'All these years,' said Poppa. 'Waiting. Planning. And now he wants a paperweight.' Suddenly he banged both fists down on his desk. 'Dammit, he'll have a train set and lump it.'

'He won't even open it,' said Momma. 'Not if I know Gaylord.'

They found a paperweight in an antique shop in town. It was a cast-iron stag, painted a revolting, dingy brown, and Poppa decided, as he carried it to the car, that it weighed about half a ton. 'If you ask me, this will go straight through the foot of any stocking,' he said. 'We'd better fix him up with some sort of wire container.' Being more than usually depressed, he decided to get it all over at once. 'I suppose we've had to invite Bea and Ben the Flower Pot Men, as usual?'

'No,' said Momma. 'They invited themselves.'

Jointly or severally, Great Aunt Bea and Great Uncle Ben were the life and soul of any party. As such, they were feared, mistrusted, and disliked by the entire family. Poppa, festooned with parcels like a Christmas tree, said wistfully, 'Couldn't Christmas be a lovely holiday if one let it. Church in the morning, stuffing oneself to repletion, catching up with one's reading in front of a huge fire, having a dignified booze-up, and bed, with a long walk on Boxing Day morning to follow.'

'Oh, and I suppose Rose's Mr Roberts will be coming,' said Momma, who had the happy knack of switching her mind off whenever Poppa became too verbose.

'Instead of which we play games that everyone detests, and fill the house with people from whom, if they were casual acquaintances in a hotel, we should flee as from the plague.'

'I wouldn't call having Bea and Ben filling the house with people,' said Momma, who had the even happier knack of making suitable replies with her mind still switched off.

'Wouldn't you?' Poppa sounded bitter. 'Stick those two in a room and it's crowded, quite regardless of numbers.' He dropped a parcel, stooped to pick it up and dropped two more. He was enraged. 'I suppose we've got Dickens to thank for all this damned Dingley Dellery,' he shouted.

'People are looking at you, dear,' Momma said. 'Don't let professional jealousy get the better of you.'

Poppa was silent. One of the dropped parcels had been the paperweight, and he was filled with sorrow at the thought of what it might have been.

'Hello, Ben. Hello, Bea. You've arrived then,' said Grandpa. He sounded depressed.

Uncle Ben slapped him on the back, a liberty even the bravest would have thought twice about taking. 'You're looking down in the mouth, John. What's the matter? *Anno Domini* catching up?' he roared.

Poppa came in, saw the visitors. 'Oh, God,' he muttered. 'And a Merry Xmas to one and all.'

Uncle Ben studied him, stroked his own plump chin. You could tell by the twinkle in his eyes that something rich was coming. 'Here, what's the matter with you, Joss? You look as though you'd seen a ghost, as the girl said to the medium.'

'The ghost of Christmas Present,' said Poppa. He didn't think it was funny. But Uncle Ben did. He roared. 'Hear that, Bea? The ghost of Christmas *Present*. *Christmas* Present, see. I say, Joss, you'll have to put that in one of your books.'

If there was anything Poppa abominated more than being called Joss, it was being told he ought to 'put that in one of your books'. It sounded, as though one composed a book like the three witches chucking their various bits and pieces into the cauldron. 'Listen,' he wanted to say. 'Do you know how William Faulkner described the aim of the writer? "To create, out of the materials of the human spirit, something that did not exist before!" That's what writing a book means. Not stringing together inanities from vapid conversations.' But he didn't say it. Uncle Ben wouldn't have understood anyway.

Rose faded into the room. 'Hello, dear,' cried Auntie Bea. She kissed Rose, then held her at arm's length like a skirt she was wondering whether to have cleaned. 'You're looking peaky, dear. Ben, isn't Rose looking peaky?'

'Yes,' said Ben, who liked them plump himself, and anyway thought the whole damn family was looking peaky.

How she hated Christmas, thought Rose. All herded together, everyone terribly hearty, alcohol simply making her feel sick and the rich food making her bilious. And Bobs was coming tomorrow and she knew she would have a wretched day, because Becky just wouldn't be able to keep her hands off him.

But at this point in her thoughts Becky made her entrance. She was soft, powdery, pink, and white. Cut into small squares she would have looked like marshmallow. She was wearing a pretty blue frock, and showing quite a lot of what Gaylord thought of without interest as that hollow bit in Auntie Becky's chest. 'Why, it's Uncle Ben,' she cried.

Up till now the family's air of stunned resignation had been having a flattening effect even on Ben. He had seemed slightly punctured. But now he looked as though someone were working on him with a foot pump. His cheeks were smooth and round, he blew out his chest, he was inches taller than a moment ago. When you got to his age a pretty little niece was something you appreciated having around. It was the only chance you got to kiss anything under sixty-five. 'Becky,' he cried, holding out his arms.

She tripped across and kissed him fondly. He reciprocated. His manner was avuncular but only just. 'It *is* nice to see you, Uncle Ben,' Becky said, rubbing her cheek against his. 'And you, Auntie Bea,' she added with the more restrained enthusiasm she kept for her own sex.

But Auntie Bea's attention was elsewhere. 'Here's my pickle,' she cried, beaming at Gaylord, who had barged inadvertently in and was now realizing that it was too late to barge inadvertently out again. He stood, looking chagrined.

43

'Well, haven't you grown,' cried Auntie Bea. 'You'll soon be as big as your Uncle Ben.'

Gaylord stuck his lower lip out.

'Aren't you going to give your old Auntie a kiss?'

Not if he can see any possible way out of it, he isn't, thought Poppa. But aloud he said, 'Gome on, Gaylord. Let's have a little social *élan*.' Not that he really cared; but Momma had just come in, and he thought he'd better go through the motions.

But Gaylord was saved by the telephone bell. Becky answered it. She held the receiver out to Rose. 'It's for you, dear. A *man*.'

Rose fluttered across. 'Hello. Rose? This is Bobs.'

'Hello, Bobs.' Rose felt as though she were acting a part on the stage, so many interested eyes were upon her.

'I'm awfully sorry, Rose, I'm afraid I can't make it tomorrow.'

Oh, no. 'Can't you really?' she said sadly.

'No. This chap's turned up, you see.'

'What chap?'

'Chap I was at Training College with. His scooter broke down near here. Couldn't get it repaired till after the holiday. So he remembered me, looked me up. He's spreading his sleeping-bag on my floor.'

'Oh, Bobs. I was looking forward to having you here.'

'Sorry, old girl. I'm afraid I'm lumbered with the chap.' He sounded damnably cheerful.

Then she had a wonderful idea. 'Bobs, bring him along. We'd love to meet your friend.'

She listened in agony to the silence. Perhaps there was no chap with a scooter. Maybe Bobs just wanted an excuse not to come. Then Bobs said, 'Well, he's not really a friend. He isn't my type at all, really.'

'You could still bring him,' she said.

'OK. But he's a bit heavy going. Never speaks till he's spoken to.'

'Don't worry,' she said. 'You'll come, then?'

'Right ho!' he said. 'See you on the Christmas tree.' And rang off.

She put down the receiver. Everyone tried to pretend they hadn't been listening. 'Mr Roberts will be bringing a friend,' she said composedly. 'I do hope no one minds.' He was coming. Nothing else mattered.

'And who is Mr Roberts?' asked Bea, archness in every fibre of her excellent tweeds.

'Auntie Rose's lover,' explained Gaylord.

'Rose, dear. Congratulations,' cried Auntie Bea. She sounded delighted, which was nice, and quite astonished, which was depressing. 'And now,' she said, 'what about that kiss my little pickle was going to give his old Auntie?'

Chapter 5

The afternoon slipped into a leisurely Christmas Eve. The nuts were rich with all the sweetness of Autumn, the port glowed red, the Benedictine mellow and amber, the cigar smoke lay in folds like linen, the fire grumbled in the hearth; after a time even Uncle Ben's funny stories began to seem faintly amusing. Then it was bedtime. Off they went one by one, each to his little nightly death. All except Momma and Poppa. Momma and Poppa went to Midnight Communion.

Walking home, in the first hour of Christmas morning, they were silent as only those who are very close can be silent. It was typical Christmas weather, warmer than Easter, drier than Whit. The air was soft and mild on their faces. In the western sky a young moon trailed a white gossamer of cloud. The heavens were a haze of stars. They came home, to the shaded lamp and the dying fire. 'Want a cuppa?' asked Momma.

They drank their tea in the half-darkness. 'Doesn't seem a year since last time,' he said.

'No,' said Momma.

He put down his cup. 'You go to bed. I'll just see to Gaylord's stocking.'

Gaylord had long ago ceased to believe in Father Christmas. And it surprised him very much to find that Momma apparently still did. He wasn't surprised that Poppa did. Poppa believed anything he was told, so long as it suited him. But that Momma, who could never accept the simplest statement without taking it to pieces, that Momma should unquestionably believe anything so absurd was really amazing.

The odd thing was that, though one no longer believed, the presents still arrived. This rather puzzled Gaylord. It couldn't be Father Christmas. It couldn't be the parents, because they still believed in Father Christmas. By a careful process of elimination he came to the decision that it must be either Grandpa or God. And there he left it; for to Gaylord, Grandpa and God were pretty well interchangeable. They were both as old as Time, they were both as near omnipotent as makes no matter, they both needed watching. So he hung up his pillowcase, happy in the knowledge that some person or Deity would fill it for him.

Poppa got Gaylord's presents off the top of the wardrobe, and went and filled the pillowcase. Gaylord was sprawled on his stomach, maintaining a high whistling note reminiscent of London Airport: Poppa came back to the bedroom. 'I wonder whether he believes in Father Christmas,' he said.

'Gaylord? Of course he doesn't. Several times when I've mentioned the old gentleman I've seen him wondering whether to disillusion me. But he hasn't. I think he's probably decided it's wiser to keep us in ignorance.'

'Why?'

'I don't know. Something far too subtle for us to understand, I'm sure.'

She was sitting up in bed, smiling at him a little tiredly. He unfastened his tie, kicked off his slippers, wound his watch. He was a haphazard un-dresser. He went and pulled aside the curtains, peered out. 'I enjoyed the Service,' he said.

'So did I. If you don't hurry you'll have to start dressing for breakfast before you've finished undressing for bed.'

But he was still gazing out of the window. 'Strange, isn't it,' he said. 'The old magic. It still works. Not always. Not often. But sometimes. Perhaps one year in ten.'

He opened the window and leaned out. Somewhere, in the quiet countryside or in his mind, a horse whinnied, there was the clash of a Roman spear, the thin crying of a child. It was Christmas Eve, in England, and the traffic was roaring down the M1, and they were dancing in Berkeley Square. It was Christmas Eve, in Bethlehem, and the Star hung low in the east, and a harp string sounded, plangent, among the stars. The child was still a child in its mother's arms, and the Cross was not yet, and two thousand years had faded and dissolved in the starlight.

He shut the window. 'It's worked this year,' he said, thinking how one day he would write a play about those dark, winter days; hearing already the shouts of the sentries, the tumult of the inn, the distant echo of the angel song ringing in the streets of the high, rocky little town.

May said, 'It's lasted well. Either something happened that was eternally essential for man. Or man invented something to fulfil an eternal need. You'll catch cold if you don't come to bed.'

'Either sounds plausible,' said Jocelyn. Lord, he thought, what a mystery it all is. He was still gazing out of the window. But he could see nothing, outside. All he could see was the reflection of the pleasant room, and of himself, and of May still sitting up in bed, still smiling. And there is another mystery, he thought. This woman who, until ten years ago, was a complete stranger, and is now flesh of my flesh. This flesh that is also spirit, and laughter, and kindliness, and understanding. This spirit that is warm, responding flesh. This wife, who, like all good wives, is mother, friend, companion, mistress. This blessed gift.

'Come to bed,' she said.

He turned, gave her his slow, anxious smile. Then he put out the light, got into bed; and from where he lay he could see the stars crowding against the window, and the luminosity where the moon had gone down into the mist.

Waking, Gaylord remembered it was Christmas with mixed feelings. It looked as though he would have to spend the entire day finding ways of avoiding Great Aunt Bea. He had never known such an insatiable kisser. He accepted normal kissing as one of the minor inconveniences, like rain or going to the loo. But with Auntie Bea the thing had got out of hand. You'd go into a room and there she'd be, waiting to pounce and enfold like a great, tweedy bear. And why did she always have to say, 'Hello, pickle'? He'd given very careful consideration to the riposte, 'Hello, chutney'. It seemed to him pretty clever. But he knew unfailingly that to Momma it would simply be Rude and Cheeky. And whenever Gaylord said anything which Momma classed as Rude and Cheeky he just felt a heel. It was quite illogical, of course, and he'd fought against it. But he couldn't help it. He just felt a heel.

Meanwhile, however, there were pleasanter things to think about. At the foot of his bed was one of the most exciting things ever devised by the fallen sons of Eve – a pillowcase stuffed with Christmas presents. Gaylord rose, tramped across the bed, and emptied it out on to the eiderdown. An apple, an orange, a new penny, a sugar mouse, and a dozen assorted parcels.

Which would be the paperweight? Taking alternate bites of apple and sugar mouse, Gaylord considered. But you just couldn't tell. He started at the beginning.

A drum. Promising. A tattoo on that in the early morning in Grandpa's room would be even more satisfying than drawing the curtains.

Meccano. Gaylord was always slightly sceptical about Meccano. You never ever seemed to get enough to build that Eiffel Tower with the light on top.

A trumpet. Better and better. If he could manage this and the drum at the same time, *and* achieve the element of surprise, he might get a 'God damn it all to hell' out of Grandpa one of these mornings.

A small iron horse with two little bushes growing out of its head. It didn't seem to do anything, anything at all. There was nowhere to wind it up. If you pressed it, it didn't squeak. He went and tried floating it in the bath. It sank like a stone. Of all the tomfool presents, thought Gaylord. Auntie Bea, without a doubt.

It was about time he came to the paperweight, now. There weren't many parcels left. He was getting anxious. He didn't think God or Grandpa could make mistakes, but you never knew. Feverishly he tore the remaining parcels open. No paperweight.

Gaylord didn't often cry, except as a matter of policy. But he cried now. The thought that at any moment he was going to have that smooth loveliness all to himself had been wonderfully exciting. To find the vision false was unbearable. He wept without restraint.

'Gaylord's crying,' Momma said, using her elbow. 'Go and see what the trouble is.'

'Hell,' said Poppa, surfacing. 'Merry Christmas, darling.' He kissed her, rolled out of bed, floundered into a dressing gown and slippers, and reeled into Gaylord's room. He remembered it was Christmas Day, and that he would be expected to be hearty and jovial for the next eighteen hours. So he might as well start now. 'What? Gaylord in tears, and on his wedding morn?' he cried, the life and soul of this six a.m. party.

Gaylord sniffed. 'It isn't my wedding morn.' He brightened. 'Is it?' he asked hopefully.

'Not really,' said Poppa. 'We couldn't find anyone suitable. Why are you crying?' he asked.

'There isn't a paperweight,' said Gaylord.

'There is, you know,' Poppa said confidently. Dammit, he'd put it there himself.

'Where?' Gaylord asked sulkily.

Poppa began scrabbling through the paper in which he and Gaylord were both knee-deep. He found the stag. 'Here, what's this?' he asked triumphantly.

'I don't know,' said Gaylord. 'What is it?'

Poppa sighed. 'The question was rhetorical.'

'What's rhetorical?'

'Never mind that,' said Poppa. '*This* is your paperweight.'

'That's not a paperweight. It's a horse with trees.'

'It's a stag.'

'You said it was a paperweight.'

But Poppa was wiping his hands on his handkerchief. 'It's wet,' he said, surprised.

'I tried floating it in the bath. It sank,' Gaylord said accusingly.

God, thought Poppa. What a conversation for six in the morning. 'Of course it sank,' he shouted. Christmas, he reminded himself. Peace on Earth. He said patiently, 'If you

51

want something you can float in your bath, one of the *less* suitable things to ask for is a paperweight.'

'I didn't want it to float in the bath.'

'But you just told me –'

Gaylord said reasonably, 'If you get something you don't know what it is, you *always* float it in the bath.'

'Not paperweights,' said Poppa.

'It isn't a paperweight,' said Gaylord.

This is where we came in, thought Poppa. He was cold, and tired. He sat down on the bed. 'This is a paperweight in the form of a stag. A stag is a male deer. Those things growing out of its forehead are not trees. They are antlers.' He felt very conscientious.

But Gaylord was losing interest. 'Would you like me to play my drum?' he enquired.

There was a silence. 'Not now,' said Poppa. 'Others are sleeping,' he added enviously.

Rose was awakened by a very uncertain trumpet. Christmas, she thought with misgiving, and Bobs and his mysterious friend coming. She would spend the day fending Becky off: there was no doubt about that. It was going to be a battle. And she had so few weapons to fight with. No looks to speak of, she thought wretchedly; and she knew she was as prickly as a hedgehog whenever she was on the defensive. I must be calm, she told herself firmly. I mustn't let them rattle me.

Christmas, Grandpa thought with satisfaction. Well, he'd always enjoyed his food, thank God, and Christmas was a time when you could enjoy it with a clear conscience. And the wine. How some people could denigrate this choicest of God's gifts he simply didn't know; but he had a feeling that when they got over on the Other Side they would find themselves listening to a few home truths about ingratitude.

Food, wine, and comfort. Grandpa was going to have a good day, provided only that that woman Bea didn't start dragooning everyone into enjoying themselves.

Christmas, thought Great Aunt Marigold. That had been a good year, when they all went skating on the lake. 'Ninety-six, had it been? 'Ninety-eight? And those other Christmases when there wasn't much coal and still less food, and not much to do except to go on knitting for the boys in the trenches, and hope the gas light wouldn't fade to show the Zepps were coming. Yet they'd been happy, those austere Christmases of long ago, happy in their strange, dreamy, end-of-the-world way. But it hadn't been the end of the world. There had been oh, so many Christmases since then. Mild ones, wet ones, frosty ones, snowy ones. And all happy. Marigold had enjoyed them all in her quiet, self-contained, mousy little way. And she was going to enjoy this one.

Christmas, thought Becky, and three young men in the house. She stretched luxuriously, flexed her claws, and purred.

Gaylord wandered round the stack yard, fancying a word with Abdullah the Turkey. No Abdullah. He went into the paddock. The same. It was unprecedented. He went into the house, where most of the family seemed to be gathered for a quiet glass of sherry. 'I can't find Abdullah anywhere,' he said.

No one said anything. 'Where *is* Abdullah?' he asked.

'In the oven,' Grandpa said unfeelingly.

Gaylord felt quite queer. It is disturbing, when you have been looking forward to a chat with someone, to find they are in the oven. He said 'Oh,' quietly.

Rose said, 'That was a cruel thing to say, Father.'

'It was?' Grandpa looked startled. 'Good Lord.'

'You must try to remember that his mind is still terribly vulnerable. It's unformed, a prey to any and every – '

'Terribly sorry,' muttered Grandpa. 'Terribly sorry. Wouldn't – not for worlds – '

'I wonder if he's got to heaven yet?' said Gaylord.

'Who?'

'Abdullah.'

'Turkeys don't go to heaven,' said Poppa.

'Do they go to hell?'

'They don't go anywhere.'

'Only down Red Lane,' chortled Auntie Bea, in what Gaylord thought execrable taste. 'Eh, pickle?'

It was too much: 'Chutney,' said Gaylord. But he only said it with his lips. He kept the sound back.

Even so, Momma gave him one of her looks. Didn't miss a thing, that woman. The sherry glass had just been touching her lips. She lowered it. 'What did you say, Gaylord?'

'Nothing, Momma.' A touch of indignation, not overdone. Just because your lips moved it didn't mean you'd said anything, did it? Some people were too apt to jump to conclusions.

Momma went on looking at him. Then she put the glass to her lips. She had a habit of closing her eyes for a moment when she drank. She did this now. 'Chutney,' Gaylord said with his lips. Momma opened her eyes and she was still looking at him. He gazed back, as bland as a Chinaman. You win, thought Momma. But don't overreach yourself, Sonny Boy.

You win, thought Rose bitterly. For Becky's timing was excellent. When Bobs and his friend arrived she was dead centre under the mistletoe. 'Hello, Becky,' said Bobs. 'Merry Christmas.'

'Merry Christmas, Bobs.'

He looked at Becky. He looked at the mistletoe. He advanced. Becky, realizing suddenly where she was standing, made to escape. Too late. He kissed her warm, red, laughing lips. 'Hello, Rose,' he said over Becky's shoulder.

'Hello,' said Rose.

He disengaged himself with obvious reluctance. Rose wanted to go and take her turn under the mistletoe. But short of dislodging Becky with a side tackle it was impossible. And now Bobs was coming to more serious matters. 'This is Stan. Stan Grebbie. Rose. Becky.'

'Pleased to meet you, I'm sure,' said Mr Grebbie, looking as though he meant it. He insisted on shaking hands. His grip was limp and damp. 'I do trust I am not intruding,' he said.

'Not at all,' said Becky. 'Any friend of Bobs – '

Anything in trousers she means, thought Rose. But she knew Becky must be feeling disappointed. Mr Grebbie wasn't likely to be *her* cup of tea. He was rising forty, and as grey as they come. Grey hair, grey complexion, grey suit, grey personality. And he was the first man she had ever met who seemed more interested in Rose than in Becky. In fact he looked as though he would run a mile if Becky took a step towards him. But to Rose he said, 'Bobs tells me you are a teacher, too.'

She smiled, at ease for once. 'It's an awful job, isn't it.'

He smiled back, a slow, defeated smile. 'Awful.'

Bobs said, 'You've got to be firm. Show 'em who's boss.' He flashed his teeth at Becky. 'Then it's all right.'

Grandpa stumped into the hall. 'Why, Mr Robson! A merry Christmas to you.' He shook hands vigorously, then looked at Bobs anxiously. 'Haven't got to dash off, have you? Time for a glass of sherry?'

'I – I,' began Bobs. But Rose said, 'Mr Roberts has come to spend the day with us. I *told* you, Father.'

'Two baleful, yellow eyes swung round and fastened on her. 'Never! No one told me No one ever does. It just happens to be my house, but as far as I'm concerned it might as well be a blasted hotel. Comings and goings – ' He turned back to Bobs. 'Delighted to have *you* of course, my dear fellow.'

Mr Grebbie had been trying, pretty effectively, to merge into the encircling gloom of the hall. But now, to his alarm, he found Grandpa's eyes fastened on him. 'No need to skulk in the shadows, young man,' Grandpa said kindly. 'Come and let's have a look at you.'

Mr Grebbie advanced an inch or two, smiling nervously. Rose said, 'This is Mr Grebbie, the friend of Bobs whose scooter broke down.'

'I suppose I knew all about that too,' Grandpa said sarcastically.

'Yes.' Rose sounded belligerent.

Grandpa gave her a look. 'Nonsense. Still, I suppose I'm an old man. Stick me in the chimney corner, don't bother to consult me about anything.'

'I *did* tell you,' said Rose.

'My dear girl, are you suggesting I'm ga-ga? Never mind. Welcome to Liberty Hall, young man. You're one of Becky's, I suppose. Ah, well, the more the merrier.' He linked his arm in Bobs' and moved off into the drawing room. Becky went with them, but Rose felt a nervous pawing at her sleeve. She turned and looked into the anxious, appalled eyes of Mr Grebbie. 'I – I really don't think I ought to stay,' he said.

Rose gazed at him. And a strange thing happened. She was suddenly filled with a great surge of tenderness. Here was someone even less prepossessing, even less well equipped for living, than herself. In her effort to reassure him she spoke with a confidence she could but rarely achieve. 'Of course you must stay, Mr Grebbie. My father is really the kindest of men. He would be most distressed if he thought he had hurt you in any way.'

He was still looking worried. 'I'm afraid I'm – not very socially minded. People like your sister and your father – awfully nice of course – but they rather terrify me.'

'I'll look after you,' she said, smiling.

'Well, if you're really sure it's all right. But I do hate butting in like this.'

'Of course you're not butting in,' she said. 'Come on. Let's go before they drink all the sherry.' She was suddenly vivacious, happy; all her heaviness was falling from her. Her maternal instinct, buried under the bric-a-brac of the years, had suddenly found an outlet, and was pushing up into the sunshine.

Chapter 6

Gaylord was aggrieved. He'd be jolly glad when Christmas was over. First, the administrative slip-up over the paperweight. Then Great Aunt Bea had spent the morning pursuing him like an overweight wood-nymph. Then they'd eaten his friend Abdullah. And he hadn't even been *nice*. Gaylord's favourite menu was shepherd's pie and rice pudding. And the sooner they got back to that and stopped eating his friends the better, he thought. And all the talk! Grandpa, carving-knife poised, whispering to Poppa. But Gaylord had heard. 'Will Gaylord want any? He seemed so upset –' And Poppa: 'Good Lord, yes. *He* wouldn't turn a hair if it was Momma trussed up on the dish.' Well it just wasn't true. *He* wouldn't want to eat Momma. He bet she'd be stringy. *And* bitter. Poppa, he felt, sometimes made some very unjust statements.

Nevertheless, this had opened up a new and rather delightful train of thought. 'Why don't we eat people?' he asked.

Grandpa, slashing away at Abdullah said, 'We probably should if we hadn't so many sheep and cattle. It's just a question of supply and demand.'

'I don't know whether you're right. Father,' Poppa said. 'People who've tried human flesh say it's not very appetizing. Rather chewy and tasteless.' He saw with alarm the dreaded twinkle in Uncle Ben's eyes. 'Do you know what the cannibal said to the missionary?' asked Uncle Ben.

No and I don't want to, thought Poppa. He hurried on, just to quieten Uncle Ben, 'But I dare say it depends on the cooking. I don't suppose these primitive tribes have ever got much beyond a simple human stew, served up cold in coconut shells.'

'Oh, my God,' said Momma.

Gaylord said with relish, 'I bet fingers aren't half *gristly*.'

'They don't eat the fingers,' Poppa said.

Grandpa said, 'That's probably one of the reasons why cannibalism has never really caught on. There's so much that is simply not edible.'

To everyone's surprise Mr Grebbie said, 'The human liver is quite revolting.'

'Tried it, have you?' asked Grandpa, passing him his portion of Abdullah.

'Oh, goodness, no,' said Mr Grebbie, flustered. 'I – just read it somewhere.' He retired into silence, amazed at his own recklessness.

'Does anyone,' asked Momma, 'still feel like Christmas dinner?'

'Not me,' said Becky. 'Who started all this, anyway?'

Everyone looked at Gaylord, who said, 'It'd be all right *minced*. Then you could put all the gristly bits in, fingers, toes, ears –'

'Be *quiet*,' Momma said.

Yes, it had been an interesting discussion, giving him much food for thought. But now dinner was over and everyone was either sitting with that awful glazed look grown-ups assumed after a meal; or sleeping. Gaylord felt instinctively that neither his drum nor his trumpet would be particularly welcome. He decided to do his disappearing act.

He found Willie in the lane. 'Let's go and look at your treasure,' he said.

They set off. 'You have many presents?' asked Willie.

Gaylord had realized that Christmas presents, from whatever spiritual or temporal source they came, were in direct ratio to the wealth of one's parents. So it wasn't likely Willie would have had many. With natural delicacy he said, 'Not much. Just a stag.'

'What's that?'

'A sort of horse.'

'What's it do?'

'Nothing,' said Gaylord.

Willie thought this over. 'Don't sound much,' he said.

Gaylord said, 'Did you have anything, Willie?'

Willie shuffled on, staring ahead. He did not seem to have heard the question. Gaylord wished he hadn't asked it.

They came to the hut. The nest of grass and leaves was scattered about the floor. The grate was empty. The lovely, lucent bauble was gone.

For a long time Willie stood with his arms hanging down, motionless, just staring. Then he was down on his hands and knees, searching, scrabbling, like an animal, grunting and sobbing and snuffling. Gaylord watched him from the doorway with a strange, sick horror. This wasn't fair. It shouldn't have been allowed to happen to Willie, who hadn't had any Christmas presents and was only ninepence to the shilling anyway. Gaylord was beginning to wonder whether God was quite as efficient as He was generally made out to be.

Willie straightened up. His nose was running, his cheeks were blotched with tears, his mouth hung loose. His voice was so slurred that Gaylord could barely understand. 'Where is it? Wha' yer done wi' it?'

Gaylord was frightened. 'It isn't me. I didn't take it, Willie.'

'Where is it?' Willie repeated. It suddenly occurred to Gaylord that the distance between them was much less than it had been. He forgot about being sorry for Willie and concentrated on self-preservation. He turned and ran.

But Willie was after him, with slow, heavy strides, panting and sobbing. Gaylord's legs began to feel as though they were made of water, with great lead weights for feet. He remembered that Willie had said, 'I shall kill you if – ' He tried to urge himself on faster, but he was at full stretch. Then his wrist was caught in a hot, rough grip. His arm was wrenched up behind his back, 'Wha' yer done wi' it?' and with each slurring syllable his arm was given another jerk.

The pain was unbelievable. It ran through his whole body like a consuming fire, it filled the whole world. There was nothing now, nothing in heaven and earth, neither Momma nor Poppa, neither sun nor moon, God or angels, life or death. Only this bonfire of pain, in which he was shrivelling and twisting like dry paper.

'It wasn't me,' he screamed. 'It wasn't me.'

Willie let go. He had stopped crying, now. He squatted down, staring out over the countryside with a look of utter hopelessness. For Gaylord, heaven and earth slowly returned. The pain was still there, coming in great surges, but an ebb was setting in. The pain no longer filled the whole world. Now was the time to run for it. But he didn't. Though his arm was hanging limp, and he knew he would never use it again; though he was still dazed by what he had just learnt about the nature of pain; yet he could not run and leave Willie alone in the winter's dusk. He stood there, sturdy legs planted wide apart, one hand gripping his shoulder. 'Who else knew it was there, Willie?' he asked.

Willie stared into space. 'You must have shown it someone,' Gaylord said.

'Wha' did yer want to go and take it for?' muttered Willie.

'I didn't. Someone else must have known it was there.'

'I'll kill whoever it was,' Willie said, his eyes blank and far away. He was absolutely still. Only his fingers moved, clawing together as though they were already round the throat of a victim. 'I'll kill you if it was you.'

'But it *wasn't*,' said Gaylord.

'I'll tell our kids,' said Willie

Gaylord felt a cold emptiness at his middle. Willie had half a dozen brothers. They were without exception cruel, vicious, and ruthless. Though they would not lift a finger to help Willie, they would seize on any excuse, such as the present one, to harass someone weaker than their collective selves. Gaylord, with the instinct of a child, sensed all this, and was afraid. If Willie told his brothers, then Gaylord knew he would really be in trouble.

But that was for later. He said, 'I've got to go now, Willie.' He took a step away. Willie rolled over, grabbed at his ankle, missed. Gaylord ran. After a time he looked back. Willie was lying in the dirt. There was not enough light to tell whether he was crying.

His arm was stiff, now; and it kept giving sharp stabs of pain. But he could use it. He felt a bit sick and dizzy, too, and not altogether sure that questions would not be asked. So he opened the kitchen door very quietly. No one was about. He reached the foot of the stairs unseen and unheard. He tiptoed up, reached his room, and began to play his trumpet.

He did it with infinite cunning. First a few tentative little tootles, well-spaced. The sort of thing those below would hear only subconsciously. Then a little louder. Then a great, continuous blast of sound that could leave no one in any doubt about Gaylord's whereabouts. 'He's been playing that damn trumpet all afternoon,' Grandpa would say. Auntie Bea would join in, 'So he has, bless him.' And the victim would have established a pretty satisfactory alibi.

But the victim had reckoned without Momma. 'He's been playing that damn trumpet all afternoon,' Grandpa said.

'So he has, bless him,' said Auntie Bea. But Momma said, 'Gaylord is up to something. I feel it in my bones.' She marched upstairs, and flung open Gaylord's door.

The effort of so much blow, coming on top of his recent ordeal, was catching up with Gaylord. His knees felt weak, he was sweating, the room was going a bit swimmy. Over his distended cheeks his eyes were anguished. Momma said, 'Gaylord, what's the matter?'

He shook his head, went on blowing though the effort was nearly killing him.

'Gaylord! Stop that ridiculous noise and listen to me.'

He lowered the trumpet, looked at her. His bottom lip began to tremble.

She had never seen him before with his defences down. She came forward without a word, sat down on the bed, took him in her arms. For a moment he held himself stiff. Then the dark head butted into her breast. She held him for a long time, waiting for the tears to come. But they did not; only long, dreadful shudderings that racked her own body. The last light faded from the room. She touched his hair with her lips. At last: 'What is it?' she whispered.

He was silent. 'What is it?' she said again.

'Nothing,' he said.

Fear made her voice sharp. 'Gaylord, you've got to tell me.'

'Nothing,' he said, pulling away from her.

'Very well,' she said gently. 'We'll talk about it later, when you're feeling better.'

He was silent. 'Now how would you like to go to bed with a nice hot bottle?' she wheedled.

'It's Christmas,' he said, outraged.

'Right,' she said doubtfully. 'But you must tell me one thing. Are you hurt?'

'Hurt?' He looked as though he did not understand.

'Yes. Hurt,' she said with sudden anger.

'No, thank you, Momma,' he said meekly.

She looked at him. There were so many questions she wanted to ask. Instead she said, sensibly, 'I'll go now, then. Come down when you're ready.'

She paused in the doorway. 'Sure there's nothing you want to tell me?'

It was too dark to see his face. But he said nothing. She went and found Poppa. She didn't want to worry him, not at Christmas. She tried the light, literary approach. 'Gaylord has a lily on his brow,' she said.

Poppa said, 'I think *La Belle Dame* would have found him a bit young. More likely overeating.'

She couldn't keep it up. 'I'm worried, Jocelyn. He looked ghastly. Sitting up there in the half darkness, blowing that trumpet as though his life depended on it. It – it nearly broke my heart.'

'And he didn't say what the trouble was?'

'Did he hell! You know Gaylord. He's of the stuff of the martyrs.'

'I'd better have a word,' said Poppa.

She shook her head. 'No. Leave him alone. He's in trouble, and he wants to play it the hard way. He's got guts, that kid.'

He looked worried. 'Ought we to let him?'

'I don't see we've got any choice. He won't tell, not at this stage. All I know is, he'd been out. That's what worries me.'

'Meaning?'

'Willie,' she said.

Chapter 7

All over England, Christmas went on. Night fell, the curtains were drawn, the fires were built up, the cakes were cut. An unsociable nation was trying, in its dogged English way, to be sociable. Relatives, who hated the sight of each other for three hundred and sixty-four days in the year, were pulling crackers together, wearing funny hats, listening avidly to one another's operations.

At The Cypresses everyone was waiting anxiously for the evil moment when Auntie Bea would suggest Games. Becky and Peter were holding hands. Bobs and Great Aunt Marigold were discussing Rugby Football, a subject on which the old lady was surprisingly well-informed. Uncle Ben and Grandpa were dozing, and so, to all appearances, was Poppa, though as he would often explain his brain was never so busy as when he seemed half asleep. Mr Grebbie watched Grandpa like a postman watching an apparently somnolent dog, and occasionally gave Rose a shy, grateful smile. Rose thought how handsome Bobs was, and that the day was passing, and they'd never yet been alone for a moment. Why had he come, she wondered. Politeness? No, she thought sadly. Bob wasn't one to give up a day out of politeness. To see Becky, then? To eat of the crumbs that fell from Peter's table? That didn't seem very likely, either. Certainly not to discuss Rugger with Great Aunt Marigold. No. It must be for her, after all. It was just that he had a queer way of showing affection.

But she wasn't altogether convinced.

Gaylord sprawled on his mother's knee, while she read him *Winnie the Pooh* in Latin. He could not stomach the English original, but found the ponderous Latin syllables strangely satisfying. '*Vita nubeculae est fons superbiae,*' read Momma.

Grandpa stirred. 'Sounds like Latin,' he muttered.

'It *is* Latin,' said Momma.

Grandpa heaved himself up, fixed Momma with his baleful stare. 'Doesn't understand it, does he?' he barked.

'Not a word,' said Momma.

'Then why in heaven's name do you read it to him?'

'He cannot stomach the English original,' said Momma.

Grandpa thought this over. He felt there must be an answer. There was. He found it. 'Couldn't you,' he said, 'find a book he *did* like? Then you could read it to him in English,' he explained.

'God knows I've tried,' said Momma.

Grandpa snorted. But he had, unhappily, started something. Auntie Bea said, 'Ah, you're awake at last, John. Now then. Who's for Consequences?'

Poppa burrowed more deeply into his chair. Stan Grebbie looked terrified. Uncle Ben sat up eagerly. 'That's right. Always play Consequences at Christmas.'

'Why?' asked Poppa, realizing the game was up.

But Auntie Bea was already dishing out pencils and paper from her handbag, refusing to take no for an answer. 'Pencil, Jocelyn?'

'I'll use my pen, thanks,' he said stuffily, producing his eight-guinea writing instrument. If he had to suffer, he'd do

67

it as elegantly as possible. 'Can I have something to write on?' he asked, holding his sheet of paper helplessly.

Auntie Bea took *Winnie Ille Pooh* from Momma and gave it to Poppa. 'I wonder you don't insist on your typewriter,' she said. She thought Poppa effete.

'Thanks,' said Poppa, sounding like a Grand Vizier acknowledging a bowstring.

The grisly ritual began. Grandpa met Miss Bardot in the Supermarket, Bobs met the Mother Superior at the Windmill, and Mr Grebbie, to his dreadful confusion, met La Pompadour on the Aldermaston March. But at last even Auntie Bea was surfeited. 'Now what?' she asked.

'Supper,' Jocelyn said promptly.

'Can't have supper yet,' said Auntie Bea. 'We've only had one game.'

Becky made a half-hearted attempt to pull her frock down over her lovely knees. 'Let's play Postman's Knock,' she said.

'Oh, be your age,' said Rose. But Uncle Ben said, 'Postman's Knock! Haven't played it for years.' He rubbed his hands gleefully and his eyes skidded over Becky's endearing young charms.

'What's Postman's Knock?' asked Gaylord.

Auntie Bea said, 'Someone goes out. Then we each choose a number and the person who's gone out calls a number and the person with that number has to go out.'

'Then what?'

'They kiss each other.'

I might have known, thought Gaylord. Talk about an obsession! He had watched Consequences with amazed incredulity, regarding it as an all-time low in adult fatuity. But he realized now that the depths still remained to be plumbed. Grown-up behaviour seldom failed to surprise and sadden him. But he was beginning to realize that until this evening he hadn't known the half of it.

'I'll go out first,' said Becky.

'I bet you will,' said Rose.

Becky went out. And called Gaylord's number.

He went into the hall. Auntie Becky was smiling under the mistletoe. When she saw who it was she went down on her knees and held out her arms. Gaylord went into them, and found comfort for his bruised body and his bruised soul. Becky was no longer smiling. She looked at him earnestly as she kissed his soft young lips. 'What's the trouble, laddie?' she whispered.

He shook his head as he clung to her, sensing something of the peace that the haven of soft and scented woman has for storm-tossed man. Then she stood up, held his head for a moment against the smoothness of her dress. Then she said, 'What number do you want?'

'Seven,' he said.

Becky gave him a friendly grin, and went back into the room. After a moment Auntie Rose came into the hall.

Auntie Rose wasn't feeling like Gaylord. 'Hello, Gaylord,' she said. 'Do you want to kiss me?'

'Not much,' said Gaylord.

'Then that's mutual,' said Auntie Rose.

'What's mutual mean?'

'It means the hell with the stupid game.'

'Oh, good,' said Gaylord, 'Do you want me to tell them a number?'

'I suppose you'd better,' Rose said, sounding nonchalant. 'Five.'

Gaylord wandered back. Rose waited. The door opened. Stan Grebbie edged his way into the hall, looking as scared as a Victorian bride on her wedding night. Oh, this is monstrous, thought Rose. Two grown people, suffering extremes of embarrassment just because it's Christmas and Bea and Becky want to play idiotic games. She said, 'It's all right, Mr Grebbie. We don't – have to go through with this, you know.'

He gave her that slow, pathetic smile. 'You're very understanding, Miss Pentecost. One doesn't wish to seem ungallant, of course. But we are – I am a bit old for this sort of thing, don't you think.'

'Poor Mr Grebbie,' she said. 'I'm afraid you're having a nerve-racking Christmas.' She laughed happily. It was strange how her confidence fed on his lack of confidence.

'A very *pleasant* Christmas,' he said. 'And I do want to thank you for all your kindness. You've been – a pillar of strength.'

'Me?' Rose was still laughing. 'Why, I'm the most negative person alive.'

'I don't think so,' he said. 'I think you're – a very fine person.'

The colour poured into her sallow cheeks. She seemed taller, more erect. 'That's the nicest compliment I've ever had,' she said quietly.

'But it's true,' he said. He moved to the door, stood fiddling with the knob. Several times he opened his mouth to speak. But the words did not come. 'What is it, Mr Grebbie?' she asked.

He looked at the floor. 'May I – kiss you after all. Miss Pentecost?'

She stood there smiling. She lifted her hands, palm outwards, in a little gesture of friendship. He came, kissed her very formally on the lips. 'Thank you,' he said. He held the door for her to go into the other room.

Poppa kissed Momma. They smiled. 'I still enjoy it,' she said. 'Even after all these years.'

'You do? I thought, poor old Momma, getting *my* number. She never has a change.'

'I don't want one. It's a funny thing about this game. It makes kissing your own husband feel quite immoral.'

Later they sang songs round the piano, happy songs, Christmas carols, silly, sentimental songs, nonsensical songs; sad Scottish songs full of mists and massacres, burns and bens, heartache and heather.

Then, suddenly the day was over. Everyone was happy, carefree in a way that seldom comes and does not stay long. Perhaps the wine had something to do with it; perhaps the songs, stiff with nostalgia; perhaps even Auntie Bea's silly games. And they all went out, the young ones, arms linked, out into the soft night air to see the visitors depart. Even Rose was giggly. And Mr Grebbie went so far as to hold Rose's right hand, while Bobs clung to her left. 'Get in, Grebbie,' Bobs said. Reluctantly Stan let go of her hand, climbed into the car. He peered out. 'Goodbye, Rose. Thank you so much.'

'Goodbye,' she said, absently. She turned to Bobs, who was still holding her hand. 'Goodbye, Bobs.'

'So long, Rosy,' he said, swinging her to him. 'Be a good girl until we meet again.'

She giggled happily, and let him kiss her in front of everyone. For a brief interval everything seemed simple and easy and straightforward. All the tensions and questionings and inhibitions were swept away, and she held her beloved lightly, gaily, as she had never done before, as she might never achieve again.

Chapter 8

And now Christmas was already hurrying into the past, like a lighted train swallowed up by the night. There was only the bleakness of the year's last days, when all the nasty, tiresome jobs one had so cheerfully put off until after Christmas began to rear their ugly heads; when the next thing on the agenda was January; when all one could see at the end of the long tunnel of winter were the lying promises of spring, and all the bloody-mindedness of an English summer.

And New Year's Eve itself came. If there was one day in the year Poppa really hated and feared, it was New Year's Eve. To stand on the brink of a whole year and try to peer forward into its troubles and anxieties, was almost more than he could bear. It was even worse than peering back at the indecisions and weaknesses and compromises of the dying year.

The dying year! Lord, that was a melancholy phrase. The year was dying, and a little bit of himself was dying with it. And not only of himself; of Momma, and Gaylord, and the old folk; of Becky's beauty, of Rose's dwindling store of youth; all dying. Ring out the old, but don't ring in the raw, cold new until I've fortified myself with another glass of port. For Poppa, though not a drinking man, always drank half a bottle of port on New Year's Eve. It kept out the ghosts and the foggy, foggy dew.

And this New Year's Eve he had something else to think about. Only today Momma had said, 'Darling, I *could* be having a baby.'

'Oh, no,' he had cried. 'Not another Gaylord.'

She had given him her amused smile. 'You don't sound wildly enthusiastic. You'd rather produce a fictional character any day, wouldn't you.'

'Fictional characters don't cry in the night,' he had said.

It was nearly midnight. Everyone else was in bed. Poppa sat in the firelight, smoking a cigar, watching the fire dancing through the red wine. What an exquisite thing a glass of port is, he thought. Something the shape and colour of a rose, and, looked at by firelight, something of the life of a rose. But it was more than a rose. You could not drink courage and comfort, relaxation and a temporary contentment, from the flower.

But you could from a glass. He did so, and filled it up again.

The door opened. Gaylord came in. 'I had a nasty dream,' he said.

'So did I,' said Poppa.

'Mine was lions and tigers,' said Gaylord. 'What was yours?'

'Just the future and the past,' said Poppa.

'I bet they weren't as bad as my lions and tigers,' said Gaylord.

'Maybe not,' said Poppa. 'But they were pretty awful.'

Gaylord lay back in the chair opposite his father, his hands thrust into the pockets of his dressing-gown, legs sprawling wide apart. It was a grown-up, man-to-man attitude. The attitude of an undergraduate holding forth, of a middle-aged man at the Club, of an old man, weary. Poppa, looking at him, saw for the first time the man hiding behind the small boy. A few more of these years, and Gaylord would be making love, striving with other men, drinking his port, worrying over what to do with Momma and Poppa now they were getting past it.

Gaylord's eyes were bright and alert, but the late hour had given them a look of wisdom and understanding that could not but be false in a child. Nevertheless, Poppa looked at his grave, grown-up, sturdy son, and felt that this was a rare moment of friendship and love when the barriers might, for once, be down. He said, 'Look, old chap. Your mother's awfully worried about you. What happened on Christmas Day?'

Poppa didn't often call Gaylord 'old chap'. But when he did, things happened in Gaylord's brain. Warning bells rang, and all the signals changed to red. Poor Poppa hadn't a chance. 'Nothing,' said Gaylord, looking Poppa full in the face with his long-lashed, serious, honest black eyes.

'I just thought you might like to tell me,' said Poppa.

'I went for a walk. Then I came home.'

'I see,' Poppa said, gazing into the fire. 'You went for a walk. And then you came home.' He sighed.

'That's right,' said Gaylord. He looked at his father. It wasn't often, he reflected, that you could ask Poppa a question without getting a silly answer. But tonight, he felt, the barriers might be down. 'When's the other Gaylord coming?' he asked.

'The what?' Poppa looked startled. After half a bottle of port he couldn't be sure which questions made sense and which didn't, but he had a feeling this one didn't.

'The other Gaylord. You said to Momma, "Not another Gaylord".'

Poppa said, 'You weren't supposed to hear that.'

Gaylord looked smug.

His father said, 'Momma's going to have another baby.'

Gaylord had feared this might be the explanation. He felt aggrieved. Surely in a matter that affected him so closely he might at least have been consulted. 'I shan't have to play with it, shall I?' he asked.

'You'll probably want to,' Poppa said, but without much conviction. Philoprogenitiveness was not one of his traits. He was inclined to think of babies in terms of nappies and six o'clock feeds, rather than of the renewal of the life force and blessed-is-the-man-that-hath-his-quiver-full.

Gaylord's eyes half-closed. For one sanguine moment Poppa thought he was dropping off to sleep. Then he opened them wide and said, 'Where do you get babies from?'

Oh, Lord, thought Poppa. It's come. He'd always hoped that, when it did, Momma would be on the receiving end. But she wasn't. He was. And at twelve-fifteen in the morning, and on an ocean of port.

But Momma had always said that questions must be answered fearlessly and frankly. So he said, fearlessly and frankly, 'Mothers produce them from inside their bodies.'

Gaylord laughed merrily. 'Oh, Poppa, you are funny,' he cried appreciatively.

Poppa said, 'I'm not being funny! It's true.'

But Gaylord was still rolling about in his chair with mirth. Jocelyn hadn't made such a successful remark for a long time. The only thing was, it hadn't been funny. He said, 'A baby is like an acorn. It grows in the mother's body for nine months, getting bigger and stronger. Then it is born and begins to lead a separate existence.'

Gaylord had sobered up. He was looking thoughtful, now. 'Poppa – ' he said.

'Yes, Gaylord?' said Poppa, bracing himself. Now he's going to ask what sets the process in motion, he thought. And that was the sixty-four-thousand-dollar question. He tried to remember how the motherhood books explained it.

Gaylord was wrinkling his brow. 'Poppa, how *could* that gentleman give that lady a partridge in a pear tree for a Christmas present?'

Poppa cried, 'Look, Gaylord, do you want me to teach you the facts of life or don't you, dammit?' He felt exasperated. When he'd been a boy he'd been insatiably curious about the subject. And all he'd ever got had been storks and gooseberry bushes. Yet here was Gaylord, having the facts served up to him fearlessly and frankly on a platter, and he lost interest. He damn well lost interest.

Gaylord said, 'Poppa, you're not listening. He couldn't have, could he? If he'd carried the tree round to her house, with the partridge in it, the partridge would have flown away, wouldn't it.'

'I don't think it's intended to be taken literally,' Poppa said. He began to get interested. 'And yet I'd never connected it in any way with symbolism, I must admit.'

'Oh,' said Gaylord. He pondered. 'I suppose he could have chained it to a bough, or something.' He rose, gazed at his father wide-eyed. 'But that would have been *cruel*, wouldn't it, Poppa.'

'Yes,' said Poppa. 'Going to bed?'

'Night-night,' said Gaylord. 'Is it next year yet?'

'Yes.' The purist in Poppa longed to explain that it could never be next year. But he was too tired.

'I bet there won't half be a lot of people *die* this year,' said Gaylord.

'Why, in heaven's name?'

'There always are,' said Gaylord. 'Millions.'

'And what have you been doing?' asked Momma, snuggling down.

'Drinking steadily. And peering into the future with Gaylord.'

'What did you see?'

'Not a damn thing, me. But Gaylord gave it as his opinion that a lot of people would die this year. He says they always do.'

'What on earth was he doing out of bed?'

'Recovering from a bad dream. Oh, and I taught him the facts of life.'

'Good Lord. How did he react?'

'Laughed his head off. Thought they were the funniest thing since Widow Twankey.'

'He may be right at that,' said Momma.

Poppa hated and feared New Year's Eve. But there were three days in the year that Rose hated and feared – the first day of each term.

Waking long before dawn she would lie, curled up knees to chin in the warm darkness, knowing that these were her last minutes of peace. Once let the alarm clock burst into strident life, and she was faced with the awful struggle of making herself get up to face another term. Each time, she thought she couldn't do it. Each time, she did. Her courage was enough to make the angels weep. But it was common. People like Rose face a firing squad every morning of their working lives.

And the winter term was always the worst. Everyone tetchy with colds, the whole school smelling of wet clothes and eucalyptus, the mornings, the awful dark mornings stark under the merciless electric light. Even the thought of seeing

Bobs again could not dispel the terror of returning to the mixed and ruthless infants on a cold January morn.

Gaylord said to Momma, 'You know that gentleman who gave a lady a partridge in a pear tree?'

'Yes,' said Momma.

'Well, he couldn't have. Because if he'd carried the tree round to her house with the partridge in it, the partridge would have flown away, wouldn't it?'

'I should think the tree would have taken a bit of handling, too, without having to keep your eye on a damn bird,' said Momma. 'Do you want a carrot?'

'Yes, please,' said Gaylord, who was helping Momma with the cooking. He munched. 'Where do you get babies from?'

'Harrods,' Momma said absently.

'Pardon?'

Momma was busy. 'Look,' she said. 'I thought you and Poppa had gone into all this?'

Gaylord gurgled. 'Poppa said they came out of ladies' bodies. He *is* funny, isn't he.'

'He's dead right,' Momma said, starting on the potatoes. But it was no good. She dried her hands, sat down at the kitchen table. 'You live on a farm,' she said. 'You know about animals. Well, humans are just the same.' She took Gaylord's hand. 'I'm going to have another baby, Gaylord. And I'm just the same.' She was really doing rather well. She felt quite touched. 'It's all perfectly natural.'

Gaylord's mind had flown to Bessie the sow. You mean you – litter?' he asked.

Momma was silent. 'Yes,' she said at last. 'Not quite the word I should have chosen. But – yes, I suppose so.'

Gaylord looked at Momma with a new interest, even a new respect. He'd never thought of her being able to do things like that. 'Can I watch?' he asked eagerly.

'No,' said Momma.

'Grandpa let me watch Bessie,' said Gaylord, disappointed.

Momma said, 'Though biologically Bessie and I may be one, there are, I hope, certain differences of temperament and sensitivity between us.'

Gaylord hadn't quite got the drift of this last sentence. He seized on one of the few words he had understood. 'What sort of differences?'

Momma said, 'Oh good heavens, Gaylord. If you can't see how I differ from an old sow I'm not going to tell you.' She stood up and went back to the sink. To her surprise she was nearly crying. She was astonished at herself. She, who was always so cool and amused, thrown off balance by a child's innocent questions. It must be this confounded pregnancy, she thought. But if I'm like this now, what am I going to be like at the end of the journey? Bessie, she reflected, would never have flown off the handle like that. Perhaps there were a few things she could learn from the old sow, after all.

Chapter 9

Now the new year was in open water and proceeding full speed ahead. The days lengthened and hardened, and thin sunshine lacquered the bare trees, the mud was thick and slab; and there began to be an excitement in the earth that spring was on the way. But then the snow came.

Snow is strange. It can be the wettest, coldest, most depressing thing in nature, as cheerless as damp bed sheets. Or it can transform the world into a magic, icing-sugar place of delight. Depending on your temperament, age, and circumstances.

Rose, cycling through it on the first morning of term, loathed it. It clogged her wheels, it was treacherous; and when her train came in, all steam and snow and moisture, it seemed more like the Trans-Siberian than the 8.32 from Shepherd's Warning.

Gaylord did not really like snow as much as everyone thought he did. You could, of course, roll one of those enormous snowballs, twice as big as yourself. But where, frankly, did it get you? He felt rather as some of the Ptolemies may have done on completion of a pyramid. It didn't *do* anything. The same could be said of snowmen. And being a sensible child he could never see the pleasure in getting a face full of snow, or of suffering agonizing hotaches in your hands, when snowballing.

Momma and Poppa loved it. They went for walks in it, scuffling it with their toes as in autumn they scuffled the dead leaves, shaking the trees so that it fell on to their laughing faces. Gaylord, whom they usually took on these ridiculous excursions, tried hard to enter into the spirit of the thing. But he found it very difficult. Parents could be a terrible embarrassment, at times.

Rose hurried to the staff-room. She looked round anxiously. No, he wasn't here yet. Outside, the snow was swirling down out of a lowering sky. It looked as though it would never, could never, stop. She began to worry about getting home. Suppose the line became blocked. What would she do? There were no buses to Shepherd's Warning. She began to feel lost, cut off from her home and family, alone among strangers.

'I wouldn't give much for your chances of getting home tonight,' said a voice. She spun round. 'Bobs,' she said.

'Got a letter,' he said. 'From an admirer.' He held it out. It was addressed to her c/o J R Roberts, Esq. 'For me?' she said. She couldn't imagine who could be writing to her. She tore it open. 'Why, it's from that Mr Grebbie,' she cried.

'Fancy,' said Bobs.

She read it and felt quite touched. 'How very nice of him. Thanking me for a happy Christmas Day. Hoping we shall meet again some time.'

'Well, well,' said Bobs.

'He was nice,' Rose said, tapping the letter against her fingers.

'You mean you liked him?' He sounded astonished. 'He's as wet as they come.'

Rose said, 'He's kind, and gentle. And I thought he was supposed to be a friend of yours.'

ERIC MALPASS

'So he is. But one must face facts.'

Rose was working herself up. Any moment, she knew, she was going to lose control. And with Bobs, of all people. But she couldn't help it. 'Well, at least he did send a thank-you letter about Christmas.'

'Meaning I didn't, I suppose?' He was beginning to look nasty. But something outside herself had taken charge now. She heard herself say, 'Well, did you?'

'I meant to,' he mumbled. 'I – just never got around to it.'

'Mr Grebbie did,' she said.

The bell went. He picked up his books, hurried off without a backward glance. 'Bobs,' she cried, miserably. He did not seem to hear. One or two people looked at her in surprise or amusement. Oh, what a fool she was. Nowadays she just couldn't help being bitchy every now and then. But to treat Bobs like that! He'd write her off as a neurotic spinster, and who would blame him? And it was the first day of term, and the Mixed Infants were either sobbing for their mums or going ga-ga over the snow. And she was certain to have a simply awful time getting home tonight, if she did get home, that is. She looked out of the window. The clouds were sagging low over the chimney pots, and the dervish-dance of the flakes made her dizzy.

At lunchtime there was no sign of Bobs. The screaming wind was piling the snow up in white convoluted drifts. There was an ominous silence where the roar of the traffic should have been. It seemed as though the winter's dusk was already occupying the town. Rose felt frightened.

By the time the final bell rang, darkness had come with a vengeance – a whirling, bewildering darkness in which sounds were blanketed and unreal, in which snowflakes stormed the street lamps like angry moths. In spite of her anxiety to get home, Rose hung about hoping to see Bobs. She must explain, apologize, try to make him see her once more as a friendly human being. But he must have got away early, for she waited until the cycle shed was empty without seeing him. What must he think of her? She longed to abase herself before him, as a penitent longs for confession. But he had gone.

Rose hurried to the station, went to her usual platform. 'Is the Shepherd's Warning train running?' she asked the porter.

'It'd have a job,' he said. He pointed to the waste of white beyond the station arch. 'Drifts twelve feet deep out there.'

'But – but how do I get home?' said Rose.

'You don't,' he said. 'There's a fire in the Ladies' Waiting Room.'

'Well, I'm certainly not spending the night there.' Rose was up in arms again. But just where was she spending the night? It was frightening not to have anywhere to go. She supposed she'd have to try the hotel. There was only one. Rose went nervously through the swing doors. She was not used to going into hotels. In the lobby a man was sitting smoking a cigar, and Rose knew that when she went up to her room he would rise casually and follow her.

But the question didn't arise. They hadn't got a room. Rose said, 'Oh dear. I'm afraid I'm stranded.'

'So are a lot of people. That's why we're full,' said the girl behind the desk. It wasn't her worry.

Rose stood and considered her next step. She was afraid the man with the cigar would come up to her with tempting offers of assistance, but to her surprise he ignored her. What could she do? She supposed the best thing was to go to the police. They'd *have* to do something.

Then she thought of Bobs. She could go to Bobs' flat, ask him to help her. After all, he might even try to run her home. And she could apologize. There, in the quiet of his flat, they could make it up again.

In the quiet of his flat! Suppose, suppose he thought she was running after him. She felt hot all over. Or suppose he tried to keep her there. After all, even dear Bobs was only a man. And everybody said that *all* men were alike when it came to – certain things.

But the thought of seeing Bobs outweighed all other considerations: that, and the thought of being no longer alone in a strange town.

She knew the flat. She'd once been to a rather miserable party there. Five minutes later she was ringing the bell.

Rose could not pretend that Bobs looked pleased to see her. 'What on earth are you doing here?' he asked, staring from the doorway.

'I can't get home. Bobs,' she said. 'The trains have stopped running.'

'Well, good Lord, you can't stay here.'

'Oh, of course not, Bobs,' she said hastily. 'I thought – I thought you might be able to suggest something.'

He thought. 'There isn't a YWCA,' he said.

The approach could hardly have been more negative. But perhaps it showed he was trying. Rose thought so, anyway. 'The hotel's full,' she said.

'Oh, gosh.' He stood to one side. 'You'd better come in, while we think,' he said gallantly.

She went in. It was a cosy little flat. The kettle was singing beside the fire. To homeless Rose it looked like very heaven. Perhaps he saw the hungry way she looked about her. 'I was just thinking about tea,' he said. 'If you'd care for some, while we think things over – '

'Oh, Bobs. Would that really be all right? I mean – I don't
want – '

'No. That's all right,' he said, rather grudgingly. 'Here, let
me take your coat.'

Rose parted with her coat with a mixture of reluctance
and excitement. Reluctance, because obviously in a bachelor's
flat the more layers you retained the safer you were.
Excitement because, well, taking off your coat in a bachelor's
flat *was* exciting.

'Poached eggs all right?' he asked.

'Yes, rather. Shall I see to the toast?'

So she sat before the fire with the toasting-fork, while the
steam rose from her shoes, and Bobs made the tea and
poached the eggs. The fire, after the cold air, brought a warm
colour to her cheeks. The excitement of this heavenly
episode brought a brightness to her eye. As they sat side by
side on the settee, eating their poached eggs in front of the
fire, he looked at her with interest. 'I think you'll have to
stay here the night,' he said. He added hastily, 'I'll have the
settee. You can have my – bed.'

The dreadful monosyllable plopped into the silence like a
stone into a deep well, terrifying Rose out of her wits. 'Oh,
but I couldn't.' She nearly dropped her plate in her agitation.
'I couldn't, really, Bobs.'

'You'd be quite safe,' he said coldly.

'Oh, I know, of course, yes. But I couldn't, really. It – it
wouldn't be fair on you.'

She might have considered that before she came here, he
thought. But she hadn't. And now he was lumbered. Still,
she wasn't too bad. The trouble was that one false, or even
sudden, move on his part, and she'd have the screaming
abdabs. Just using the word 'bed' had nearly sent her hand
over fist up the curtains. He said, quite gently for him, 'Now
I'm going to wash up. You put your feet up and relax.'

Well, Rose certainly wasn't putting her feet up. But she
did try to relax. After all, here she was with dear Bobs. She

didn't want to spoil it all, did she. So she perched on the edge of the settee with her hands folded in the lap of her sensible tweeds, and looked and felt about as relaxed as a lion tamer going solo for the first time.

Bobs came in, wiping his hands on the tea towel. He looked at her. He said, 'I hate a centre light, don't you?' He switched it off and lit a table lamp. 'Music?' he said. He started up the record player. A Strauss waltz. He threw some more coal on the fire. He sat down on the settee. Old Rose didn't look half bad in this light. Come to think of it, he was quite fond of her if only she wouldn't make all the running. And she certainly didn't look as though she would tonight. Funny creatures, some women. Chased you like mad, then when they'd got you cornered they were frightened to death. Well, they couldn't have it both ways. He reached out and took Rose's hand.

Chapter 10

Gaylord plodded home from school. Had the snowflakes been cabbage whites and he a cabbage they could not have been more attentive. They tickled his nose, they hit him in the eye, they fluttered down his neck, they lodged in his ears. And the snow was getting deep. He wasn't at all sure he would ever reach home.

His white world was as empty as Antarctica. All the familiar landmarks had gone. Only the howling of the snow wind, and the darkness coming on, and the trees bending over him.

He tried whistling to keep his spirits up. But as the only sound he could produce was a rather dreary sizzle, it didn't help much.

Something was moving ahead of him. Wolves? He peered into the snowy murk. Two forms were barring his path. And they weren't wolves. They were worse. They were Willie and his brother Bert.

They looked at him in menacing silence. Bert pulled something out of his pocket. Flick, and the knife was open. He began thoughtfully to clean his nails with the vicious point.

Gaylord watched him with dreadful fascination. At last: 'Is this the little bastard?' Bert asked.

'That's him,' said Willie.

Bert went on cleaning his nails. 'What did you pinch our Willie's thing for?' he asked.

'I didn't,' Gaylord said indignantly.

Bert looked at Gaylord then. And Gaylord shivered. For Bert's eyes held no human expression. They held neither pity nor hatred. They were just blank. 'I'll give you a week,' he said. 'Give it him back in a week, or else.'

'Or else what?' asked Gaylord, not defiant, just seeking information.

Bert stopped cleaning his nails. He held the knife and moved the point slowly towards Gaylord's face. Gaylord stood, mesmerized. The knife was an inch from his face. He could see a snowflake clinging to its bright surface, slowly melting into water. 'Else I'll do you,' Bert said.

'I'll tell my father.'

'I'll do him too,' said Bert.

Gaylord said, 'But I haven't got Willie's thing. I *can't* give it back.'

'Come on,' said Bert. He and Willie faded into the darkness.

Gaylord trudged on, very thoughtful. Two more forms loomed out of the whiteness. 'Here he is,' said Momma. She sounded relieved.

'You look like the chap in "Excelsior",' said Poppa. They fell in on either side of him. Each took a hand. Gaylord was not always unreservedly glad to see his parents. But he was tonight. In fact, he'd never been so glad to see anyone in his life, though he didn't show it, of course. He had a feeling it wouldn't be good for them.

'You're very quiet,' said Momma. 'Anything the matter?'

'I've got a headache,' said Gaylord.

Momma hated Gaylord's headaches. They could mean almost anything. 'Been failing to see eye to eye with teacher?' she asked.

'Sort of,' said Gaylord, relieved. Now Momma had placed her own interpretation on things, she would be quite happy. No more awkward questions.

And he was right. Momma and Poppa walked on, making pleased remarks about the snow, and allowing Gaylord to get on with his serious thinking.

But there wasn't much thinking to do. The facts were these: 1. Gaylord must produce Willie's thing by next Monday, or he'd be done; 2. Gaylord couldn't produce Willie's thing by next Monday because he didn't know where it was. Therefore 3. he'd be done.

It was all too simple.

He remembered his encounter with pain on Christmas Day. He felt lonely, and frightened, and bewildered. He was so scared that he even considered telling his parents. But he soon put that idea out of his mind. Momma would want to know everything. Then, when they'd got it all out of him – 'This is what comes of talking to Willie. I told you, didn't I.' On and on and on. No. There must be some other way. But what?

That night, when he said, 'And God bless Momma and Poppa and Grandpa and Auntie Rose and Auntie Becky, and Abdullah if it's not too late,' he added, 'And don't let Bert do me.' It was all he could think of.

Chapter 11

Bobs, having taken Rose's hand, slid his other arm about her shoulders. 'Cosy?' he asked.

Rose looked at him long and thoughtfully. Then, suddenly, she relaxed and smiled. It was a sad, anxious smile. It was the smile of a woman in love with a man who she knows does not love her. 'Very cosy,' she whispered.

'Good.' He kissed her.

It should have been wonderful. But it wasn't. There were too many doubts and questions. She kissed him, then, gently, thoughtfully, like someone tasting a wine she knows will be too strong for her. And it was still only six o'clock, and the long evening was before them.

The doorbell rang.

Even Rose herself could not have said whether her reaction was 'Thank heaven,' or 'Damn and blast.' Bobs said, 'Who on earth?' He went to the door.

Rose sat still, once more stiff and taut. Who could it be? Oh, don't let it be anyone she knew. She couldn't bear to be found thus, alone in a man's flat. She would give a ridiculous impression of guilt, she just couldn't help it.

But it wasn't likely to be anyone she knew. Just one of Bobs' friends, perhaps. Or someone from the next flat, come –

'I suppose you haven't got Rose here?' said a pleasant, rather husky voice. The very last voice she would have wished to hear. And then Bobs, absolutely delighted, 'Why, Becky, come on in. This *is* a pleasure.'

Becky came in, prettily muffled in a sheepskin coat. Her bright, amused eyes took in the whole situation at a glance. 'Hello, Rose. Thought you might be stranded.'

'Hello,' said Rose.

'I read your little mind like a book. I thought, Rose won't be able to get home. So she'll go to Bobs. Nowhere else in Ingerby that she can go. Aren't I clever?'

Bobs said, rubbing his hands, 'Well, now you're here you'd better take your coat off. You can kip with Rose.'

Becky's lovely eyes were full of gratitude. 'Oh, Bobs, you are sweet. But I've come to take Rose home. Peter's outside with the estate car. He's sure he can get through.'

'I'll get my coat,' said Rose. But she knew now what her reaction was. It was 'Damn and blast'.

Becky looked at the record player, which was still manfully turning out seductive music. 'Unless I'm breaking anything up,' she said. 'Don't come if you'd rather stay.'

'No. No, of course I'm coming,' said Rose. She couldn't stay now. She'd never hear the last of it. Anyway, Bobs was already holding her coat.

'I don't want to spoil love's young dream,' Becky said understandingly.

'Good Lord, no,' said Bobs.

'Don't be silly,' said Rose. She fastened her coat. 'Goodbye, Bobs. Thanks for the tea.'

'So long,' he said. 'So long, Becky.'

Becky gave him a radiant smile. Then they were gone. Rose, bouncing about in the back of the estate car, thought of the warm, lighted room she had left, and of the long evening, so full of exciting and alarming possibilities, that had been snuffed out like a candle. An evening that might never, that would never, return. And now a dreadful, unworthy suspicion was wriggling about at the back of her mind. She tried to smother it, but it would give her no peace. 'How did you know where Bobs lived?' she asked, trying to sound casual, but hearing her voice hard and hostile.

Becky lifted her head lazily from Peter's shoulder. 'I telephoned the police,' she said. 'They were awfully helpful.'

Rose said, 'You went to all that trouble? Just to help me get home?'

'Of course, dear. You'd have done the same for me, wouldn't you.'

Rose was silent. It was true, it was almost certainly true. Becky was as good natured as they come. Rose had to admit that. But in her present mood she still preferred to think it was a calculated plot to ruin her evening with Bobs. It wasn't fair. She felt terribly sorry for herself. Not only was she unattractive to start with. But every time there was a chance of her seeing Bobs something interfered: the weather, father, Becky. Always, always Becky. She sat in the chill dark, biting her lips to keep back the sound of her angry weeping, and the tears ran cold and wet down her cheeks.

They reached home without incident. Becky and Peter burst into the house. Rose followed slowly, trying desperately to conceal the signs of her weeping.

'Good, you've made it,' cried Momma. 'But there's no sign of Rose. We're worried.'

'It's all right,' Becky said. 'We've got her.' Rose came in, blinking in the brightness. 'Saved her from a fate worse than death, didn't we, Rose?'

'I don't know what you mean,' said Rose.

Becky was unfastening her coat. 'Oh, come off it. You're talking to an expert. A dim light, the settee in front of the fire – '

'Where was all this?' asked Momma, intrigued.

Rose said miserably, 'I went to Mr Roberts' flat because I was stranded. It was all perfectly respectable.'

Becky said, 'Darling, when a man puts on "Tales from the Vienna Woods", things don't stay respectable very long.'

'Bobs isn't like that,' Rose said.

'Isn't he, dear?' Becky said sweetly. For a long moment the two sisters looked at each other. It was a look frightening in its challenge. Then Rose dropped her eyes. Grandpa said, 'Roberts? Roberts? Is that the chap who came at Christmas?'

'Yes,' said Rose.

'Really? Extraordinary coincidence. Extraordinary,' said Grandpa.

'What is?' asked Poppa irritably.

'Why, Rose meeting this chap again, of course.' Really, his son could be a fool at times.

Poppa said, 'Dammit, Father. There's nothing extraordinary about it. They teach at the same school. He came here at Christmas because he's a friend of Rose's.'

Grandpa floundered in his chair like a hippo struggling to leave the ooze. 'He did nothing of the sort. He came at my express invitation. I'd met him in November. Damned interesting chap to talk to. So I asked him for Christmas.'

'Oh, I give up,' said Poppa. And Rose thought, this blasted family. It isn't enough to have my evening with Bobs ruined. Now we've all got to discuss it and get at cross purposes over it. And I can't bear it. I just can't bear to have my private life chewed over in this way. But already Grandpa was barking,

93

'Anyway, what's all this. Rose? Not going to spend the night with the fellow, were you?'

Rose said, 'I couldn't get home. The hotel was full. What did you expect me to do? Curl up in the snow?'

'Yes, but I mean to say. Spending the night with the fellow.' Grandpa looked concerned. 'Wouldn't have done in my day, you know,'

'What wouldn't dear?' asked Great Aunt Marigold.

Oh, no, thought Rose. Now Great Aunt's coming in. We shall all go back to square one.

Grandpa turned his malevolent gaze on his sister. 'Spending the night with a man,' he bellowed.

Aunt Marigold looked more interested than shocked. 'When was this, dear?'

'I didn't,' cried Rose. 'And he was going to have the settee, anyway.'

'They always say that,' Becky murmured.

'You be quiet,' snapped Rose. She was suffering terribly. This open discussion of a love affair would have embarrassed most people. But Rose was unusually shy and modest. As Grandpa had once observed to Jocelyn, 'If our Rose stopped for a pee in the middle of the Sahara, she'd go behind a sand dune.' And so she was quite overcome by confusion, and therefore, as she would have admitted, as prickly as a hedgehog. 'You be quiet,' she said again.

'Of course, dear,' Becky said meekly.

'And don't sound as though I'm asking you to hush something up,' Rose shouted.

'Hoity-toity,' said Great Aunt Marigold.

Rose said, 'Listen, all of you. I will not have my private affairs discussed in this way. It's – it's indecent.'

'Hear, hear,' said Poppa.

Aunt Marigold said, 'Your Great Aunt Maud went off with a Nicaraguan.'

'What the hell's that got to do with it?' Poppa asked.

'Mexican,' said Grandpa.

'What, dear?'

'Maud went off with a Mexican.'

'Are you sure, dear? He was a very dark-skinned gentleman.'

'Well, so are Mexicans, dammit.'

Poppa said, 'Look, Rose hasn't gone off with anyone. She simply went to a friend's because she was snowbound. Very sensible, if you ask me.'

'Thanks, Jocelyn,' Rose said. 'And now that's settled I'll go to my room, if no one objects. And I shan't be wanting any supper.' She made an exit.

Grandpa looked nonplussed. He glared at his son. 'What's the matter with her? Not been upsetting her, have you, Jocelyn?'

'No,' Poppa said angrily.

'She's a very sensitive girl. Rose. You have to be very careful what you say to her.'

Poppa shook the paper in his annoyance. 'I did *not* upset her. Father.'

'All right. All right. No need to be peevish. I was simply pointing out that she needs careful handling.'

'And I'm not being peevish.'

Great Aunt Marigold, who had been thinking about Mexicans, came back home. 'Rose seemed upset,' she remarked. 'Has Jocelyn been saying something?'

Poppa rose, flung down the paper, and marched from the room. 'A good boy, Jocelyn,' his aunt said approvingly. 'Gone to apologize, I shouldn't wonder.'

Chapter 12

England was immobilized. The snow, as always, had caught the Island Race completely unprepared. The nation's cars were stuck in snowdrifts. The nation's trains were stuck in sidings. Helicopters dropped hay to New Forest ponies and food to benighted travellers. The papers and the television could speak of nothing else. A people that had dealt so magnificently with Bonaparte, the Kaiser and Hitler was bewildered and frustrated. They felt subconsciously that anything over two inches was un-English. Like earthquakes and tornadoes, it was the sort of thing foreigners had to put up with as part of their disorganized way of life. But not us. So although they complained bitterly, they didn't really do anything about it. It shouldn't have happened, not in England. It was an error of taste. Don't look, and it will go away.

But it didn't go away; to the intense relief of at least one citizen. Gaylord, with next Monday hanging over him like doom, watched the tumbling flakes like a castaway in a small boat watching the rain. If this kept on it could save him. If this kept on, the roads could be impassable by next Monday. Or Gaylord could make out a good case for their being impassable.

But on Thursday, of course, the temperature shot up fifteen degrees, the snow turned to rain, and the country became a quagmire. The smutched and dirty snow couldn't get away fast enough. Brambles and briars stuck up again like wire on a deserted battlefield. Trees were black and dripping, and streams ran black under crusty overhangs of snow.

Gaylord watched all this with a sinking heart. He wouldn't be staying safe at home on Monday, as he had begun to hope. He would be out, alone, in the menace of the country lanes. And somewhere along the way he would meet Bert and Willie, violence and pain.

Friday came, and the sun shone, hastening the thaw.

Saturday, and a dry frost hardening the mire, drying up the roads. Sunday. Gaylord tried, by sheer will-power, to slow down the inexorable march of time. But it didn't work. Time went on, ticking, tolling the minutes and hours away. Bedtime came, and he went meekly as a lamb to the slaughter, without even an attempt at delaying tactics, which left Momma vaguely uneasy. He curled down under the sheets. It was warm and dark. He would like to stay here for ever. He tried holding his breath. But that didn't work either. Well, at least he would stay awake all night, putting *off* the moment of fear as long as possible.

But he must have dozed, for suddenly with a sick feeling of horror he heard Momma calling him to get up, and he knew that he had squandered the sweet and gentle night in sleep.

Momma came in, damnably brisk and efficient. 'Come on, Gaylord. You'll be late.'

'I've got a headache,' he said in a wan voice.

Momma paused. 'You look all right,' she said doubtfully.

'I feel sick,' said Gaylord. He did, too.

Momma put a hand on his forehead. 'I think I've got a temperature,' he said.

Momma fetched the thermometer, stuck it in. Gaylord tried to improve matters by wrapping his tongue round it. Momma waited, looking at him thoughtfully. She whipped out the thermometer, peered, 'Ninety-eight point four,' she said.

'Is that *very* bad?' asked Gaylord.

'It's dead normal.'

Gaylord fanned himself with his hand. He gasped for breath. 'I *feel* hot, anyway. I feel as hot as hell.'

'Gaylord!'

Just like Momma, believing a little glass tube rather than her own son. But she was still looking worried. 'You haven't really got a headache, have you?'

He passed a hand wearily over his brow. 'It's awful.'

'Come on. Get up,' she said.

'But I'm ill. I think I've got measles.'

'If you'd got measles we shouldn't be able to see you for spots.'

He was growing desperate. 'Teacher says you can have measles without spots. She says they're the worst sort.'

Momma sat down on the bed. She took her son's hand. 'Gaylord, why don't you want to go to school?'

'I do,' he said righteously. He wasn't falling for that one. 'But it wouldn't be fair to go and give everyone my measles, would it.'

Momma put a hand on his forehead again. Cool as a cucumber. 'It wouldn't be anything to do with Willie, would it?'

'No,' said Gaylord. It wasn't. It was Willie's brother.

'Then what *is* worrying you? Are you being bullied at school?'

'No. It's just my measles.'

'Oh, for heaven's sake!' Mother and son looked at each other. His face was as blandly innocent as always. But was there a lurking fear behind the candour of that gaze? She wished she knew. She said, gently: 'You'll have to get up and go to school, Gaylord. I'm sure there's nothing the matter with you, and if it's something you're afraid of, well, running away from it won't help.' She smiled, though she did not feel like smiling. 'That's one of the first and hardest lessons we have to learn.'

From the door she looked back. Gaylord was tumbling out of bed. Brave kid, she thought. She went back to her room. 'Gaylord's got measles,' she said. The spotless variety.'

'Meaning?' said Poppa.

'Meaning he's still scared about something, and he still won't say what.'

Poppa nodded. 'So the only thing is for him to go and face it.'

'Yes. Are we being very hard?'

'It's not us,' he said. 'It's life. That's the way it is.' He went for his bath. When he came back, he said, 'I've been thinking. I could walk with him as far as the village. Say I want some tobacco. I might learn something.'

Momma looked relieved. 'I wish you would, Jocelyn. I don't like this business. It must be something serious to worry Gaylord.'

Gaylord struggled with his breakfast. Every mouthful had to be forced down. He wished Momma would stop watching him. Then Poppa pulled out his pouch, made to fill his pipe, and said, 'Dash it, May. I'm out of tobacco. I'll have to pop into the village.' He turned to Gaylord. 'Do you think I might have the pleasure of your company?'

Had it been Momma, Gaylord would have been highly suspicious of this move. But you couldn't suspect Poppa of ulterior motives. Gaylord could read Poppa like a book. 'OK,' he said.

'Don't say OK,' said Poppa. 'Ready?'

'Just going to the toilet,' said Gaylord.

Poppa was scandalized. 'To the *what*?'

'Teacher says "toilet",' said Gaylord. He went.

Poppa turned to Momma. 'I knew this would happen. It always does. Send them to a village school and they pick up the most dreadful expressions.' He fumed. Grandpa came in. 'What's the matter with you?' he asked his son.

Poppa said gravely, 'We've just learnt that Gaylord has been taught – taught, mark you – to say "toilet" for WC.'

'Good God,' said Grandpa.

'I wouldn't have minded a bit of good, honest Anglo-Saxon,' Poppa said. 'But – toilet. I shall write to the Education Committee.'

Gaylord came back. He and Poppa went into the hall. 'Where's he going?' asked Grandpa.

'Buying tobacco,' said Momma.

Grandpa hurried to the door. 'Hey! Jocelyn! I can let you have a spare tin.'

'It's all right,' Poppa said. 'I want to go.'

'Want to? At this hour of the morning. You?' Grandpa made no secret of his contempt for Jocelyn's inability to come to life before ten-thirty.

'Yes. Me,' Poppa said angrily.

Great Aunt Marigold appeared carrying a cold hotwater bottle and an empty cup and saucer. 'Why has Jocelyn got his coat on?'

'Don't be alarmed. He's not starting to work for his living,' Grandpa said. He was inclined to bloody-mindedness on cold mornings.

'Now look here, Father,' cried Jocelyn. Almost any remark of the old man's could drive him to exasperation. But this bland assumption on the part of the whole family that a writer earned a living without working – it maddened him.

Becky shot through the hall on her way to snatch a cup of tea before her transport arrived. 'Leaving home, Jocelyn?' she inquired gaily.

'I shall be late,' said Gaylord.

'I'm coming,' Poppa said wearily. But now Aunt Marigold was insisting on embracing him fondly, or as fondly as she could with a cup and saucer in one hand and a hot water bottle in the other; though where on earth she thought he was departing to, no one knew. Rose, arriving in the middle of this affecting scene, cried, 'Jocelyn. What is it?'

Poppa said in a taut voice, 'I am not, as you might imagine, leaving to seek my fortune in the Americas. I am simply going into the village to buy an ounce of tobacco.'

'Oh, is that all?' Rose sounded disappointed.

Grandpa said, 'There's no need, I've told you. I can let you have a tin.'

'I'll bring you some from town, if you can wait till this evening,' Rose said.

Becky, rushing through the hall again, said, 'Why don't you ring up old Bates? He'll send you some with the groceries.'

'I shall be late,' said Gaylord.

'Coming,' said Poppa. He shook off Aunt Marigold and departed. What a family, he thought. I decide to walk to the village, and before you can say knife they've turned it into a cross between a Grand Opera farewell and a parliamentary debate. He strode along, fuming.

Gaylord ran by his side. He felt safe. It was a fortunate coincidence that Poppa should have decided to come into the village this morning. But it wasn't really this morning that Gaylord was worried about. It was tonight.

They reached the school. Poppa looked at the mayhem going on in the schoolyard. No wonder Gaylord got headaches at the thought of it. Poppa thought that anyone who ventured into that lot deserved the George Cross. 'Would you like me to come in with you?' he asked.

Gaylord looked horrified at the suggestion. 'No thank you, Poppa.'

'Sure you'll be all right?'

'Sure.' He went in through the school gate, and was promptly engulfed in the screaming, shouting, shoving melée. Poppa came away thoughtfully. There was a lot to be said for nearing middle-age, he decided. You at least know that, short of world war, you couldn't be plunged into that sort of dogfight.

He walked home slowly. 'Well?' said Momma. 'Did you learn anything?'

'Not a thing. But I don't wonder he had the spotless measles. I wouldn't have gone into that playground for all the tea in China. Not without a police escort.'

Momma said, 'I think that must be the trouble. He's being bullied.'

'And yet, once we were there he seemed to cheer up. He went into the jaws of death almost as though he enjoyed it.'

'I *had* been hoping you might have a word with his teacher,' said Momma.

'What? About saying toilet?'

'No, you fool. About the fact that your son is being badly frightened by somebody.'

Poppa looked sheepish. May was right, of course. He ought to have seen someone in authority. Oh, how he wished he was one of those strong, practical men who knew just what to do in a case like this. That was the sort of husband a fine woman like May deserved; not a poor, ineffectual creature like himself. He tried to think quickly, but without much effect. He was too used to choosing words and polishing sentences to be a fast thinker. Momma watched him with fond irritation, and waited to see what he was cooking up. At last: 'I'd thought I'd meet him out this evening and try to see his teacher then. I thought she'd be less busy,' he explained.

'Forgetting, I suppose, that we are catching the three-thirty to Ingerby.'

'We are?' He looked startled. 'Oh, yes. That Brains Trust thing.'

'Yes, dear. That Brains Trust thing.' Then, to his intense relief, she smiled at him. 'Strange, isn't it? We're both thought intelligent enough to go on a Church Hall Brains Trust. But when it comes to dealing with our own infant, he gets us baffled every time.'

Chapter 13

Gaylord was a railway engine, all noise and steam and flashing piston rods. He was hurtling along at a steady sixty, chuffing loudly, slowing-down a little for the dangerous bend by the coke store, then faster, faster as he went down the straight past the covered playground.

There was a small knot of boys at the end of the straight. A station, obviously. Gaylord pulled levers, turned handles, peered anxiously at dials. He was slowing down now. The chuffing became slow and deliberate, died. He came smoothly to rest beside the knot of boys. A good run, he told himself. One minute ahead of schedule.

No one took any notice of him. The boys were all looking at something that one of them was holding. Gaylord stopped being a railway engine and became an inquisitive small boy.

'Let's see,' he said.

Grudgingly they let him in. He looked. The thin, mid-morning sunlight seemed to have been caught in Sammy Breen's hand and broken into splinters of blue and red and yellow. Gaylord's mouth fell open. He was looking at Willie's paperweight.

Gaylord trembled. He could feel his hand, of its own volition, coming up to snatch this one thing that stood between himself and being done. But he knew it was no use.

Even so, he could not stop his voice crying out, 'That isn't yours. It's Willie's.'

'It is mine, then.' Sammy Breen covered it with his hand.

'Where did you get it?'

'Found it,' said Sammy. He had cropped sandy hair, shifty eyes, and an ill-tempered expression. His parents, quite unnecessarily it seemed, had told him always to stand up for his rights.

Gaylord realized instinctively that there was only one argument that would appeal to Sammy. Money. And all he'd got was sixpence. He thought bitterly of his Christmas money, all squandered on sweets, pop, and even the RSPCA dog outside the Post Office. 'I'll give you sixpence for it,' he said.

'Sixpence!' Sammy looked shocked. 'You can have it for half a crown.'

Half a crown! It wasn't a big sum. Given time to realize his assets Gaylord might have produced it fairly easily. 'I'll bring you half a crown tomorrow if you'll let me have it,' he said.

'OK,' Sammy said indifferently. 'You bring the money tomorrow and you can have it tomorrow.'

But tomorrow was too late. He'd have been done by then. 'Can't I have it today?' he said.

'Not without the money,' said Sammy. And now, under Gaylord's very eyes, young David Snow produced two shillings and sixpence and was given the paperweight. The bell rang, they returned to their classroom. David sat looking at his new treasure. Then the teacher came in. David put it in his desk. The lesson began.

Gaylord was desperate. Tonight, in the winter's dusk, Bert and Willie would be waiting for him. He felt, once more, the pain of his body being screwed to unbearable intensity. Only this time it would be worse. He saw the knife blade flashing close to his eyes. Only this time it would not stop an inch away. This time it would come on mercilessly, stabbing, slicing. When the bell rang for dinnertime he sat on. The others ran off noisily. David went with them. He had not taken anything out of his desk.

Miss Marston looked at Gaylord, wondered whether to speak to him, decided not to, and left the room. Gaylord was left with the paperweight and his conscience.

Gaylord's conscience was not very old, and hadn't had much experience. Like a learner driver it could drive a fairly straight course. But it wasn't used to dealing with emergencies. And in this particular emergency it flung up its hands like an Egyptian taxi driver and cried, 'Allah drives.'

Gaylord, bereft of conscience, went and opened David Snow's desk. The paperweight was indeed there.

Gaylord shut the desk. He couldn't steal. But it wasn't stealing, not really. It was just giving Willie his thing back.

He opened the desk again. But David had paid for it, which complicated the moral issue.

But Willie hadn't had the money. Therefore it was still Willie's. It was clear-cut.

But Gaylord knew it wasn't clear-cut at all. On the other hand, something else was very clear-cut indeed. If Gaylord hadn't got that paperweight, Bert would do him. He picked it up, put it in his pocket, and shut the desk. 'What are you doing, Gaylord?' asked a sorrowful voice.

Miss Marston was a nice woman, even if she did say 'toilet'. She loved and respected her children. And of them all she perhaps loved and respected Gaylord best. She thought him sturdy, well-mannered, and above all individual. A child of character. And here he was, looking as furtive and guilty as a common sneak thief. Which, she was very much afraid, was just what he was. 'What are you doing?' she said again. Gaylord thought his heart was breaking. 'Just – getting something,' he said.

'What?' Miss Marston's voice had a bit of an edge, now. He knew unconsciously that the old Gaylord was dead. The cheerful, self-respecting Gaylord was dead. In his place was a poor creature whom the world would know, worst of all he himself would know, as thief. That die was cast. But, he decided at the unconscious level, he wouldn't know himself as liar as well. That at least could be saved from the wreck. 'What?' Miss Marston said again, and he pulled the paperweight out of his pocket and said, 'This.'

Perhaps, she thought, there's some quite rational explanation. He couldn't be a thief, this boy. She said, 'Is it yours? Had David taken it from you?' That must be it, of course. She must learn not to jump to conclusions.

But Gaylord said, 'No, Miss. It was David's. He'd bought it from Sammy Breen.'

She cursed his honesty. 'Then why did you take it?'

'It's – pretty,' he said.

'Yes,' she said. 'It's pretty. But you wouldn't take it just for that.'

He said nothing. 'You do realize I shall have to take this further. I shall have to tell the Head.'

'Yes, Miss.'

They stood in silence. 'Well,' she said at last. 'You'd better put it back.'

He put it back, closed the desk lid. He was a caught thief, and tonight Bert would beat him up.

Miss Marston said, 'You'd better go and have your dinner. I'll see you about this later.'

'Yes, Miss,' he said, going. He didn't want any dinner.

She caught him up. 'Why *did* you take it, Gaylord?'

He stood, silent. She waited. The desire to fling her arms round this mute object of misery was almost unbearable. With a great effort she overcame it. They went out together. She, too, did not want any dinner.

Then dinner was over, and afternoon school was over, and Bert the Knife was out in the lanes waiting to pounce on Gaylord the Thief. But first the whole dreary business of the paperweight had to be gone into again. That wasn't Miss Marston's fault. It wasn't anybody's fault. It was just that one grain of dishonesty, once discovered, upsets the smooth running of many lives for an indefinite period.

But the class dismissed, and teacher had said nothing. She sat there, reading, as they filed out. Gaylord drew level with her desk. Another second and he would be past. And then: 'Gaylord,' she said quietly, still reading her book.

He checked. 'Yes, Miss?'

'Wait,' she said, still reading.

He waited. Then, when all the other children had left, she looked up. Her young face was heavy with compassion. She said, 'You know it's my duty to go to the Headmistress about this?'

Gaylord nodded.

'Well, I'm not going. Not today, anyway.'

Gaylord was relieved. He hadn't relished the thought of that female Jehovah getting her teeth in.

'Not,' said Miss Marston, 'to save you unpleasantness. But because I feel there is something behind all this, and I want to find out what it is.'

'Yes, Miss,' said Gaylord.

It wasn't the most helpful of remarks. 'So I've decided to talk it over with your parents. I thought I might walk home with you tonight.'

'Yes, Miss,' said Gaylord, less relieved. Momma was going to take some handling, he knew that. On the other hand, if Miss went home with him he'd nothing to fear from Bert. As an escort, Miss would be as effective as a posse of outriders.

They set off, saying little. And halfway home, sure enough, they met not only Bert, but all Willie's brothers. The Foggerty boys were lounging by a gate, on the loneliest part of Gaylord's walk. When they saw Gaylord they stiffened, and waited in watchful, menacing silence. Not once did one of them take his eyes off Gaylord's face. Miss Marston looked at them nervously, and faltered. But she must never, she told herself, show fear before one of the children. So she walked bravely on. Gaylord, knowing himself protected, fairly swaggered. Then, being safely past, he turned and cocked a solemn snook.

'What nasty looking boys,' said Miss Marston. 'It's a pity they haven't something better to do than hang about looking for mischief.'

They weren't looking for mischief, thought Gaylord. They were looking for me. He was already deeply regretting the cockiness that had led to his gesture of contempt.

Grandpa was in the paddock. He looked at Miss Marston with interest. Gaylord said, 'This is Grandpa.'

'How do you do,' said Miss Marston. 'I'm Gaylord's teacher. Miss Marston.'

'How do you do,' said Grandpa, wondering what the hell.

Miss Marston said, 'I've really come to have a word with Gaylord's parents. Something –'

'I'm afraid they've gone to some tom-fool entertainment in Ingerby. They won't be back till eleven.'

'Oh, dear. And I did want to see them.' Miss Marston looked distressed. A sense of disaster hung over the paddock. Grandpa, who was nobody's fool, felt it. 'You'd better come inside,' he said.

They went in. 'Now,' Grandpa said. 'Is there anything I can do?'

She looked at him in doubt. She was desperately twisting the fastening of her handbag. 'I really wanted his parents – '

'Accepting the fact that you can't see his parents, do you feel that I can help?'

Miss Marston went on twisting her handbag. For all his courtesy the old man frightened her. After all, a thunder flash looked harmless enough until you put the match to it. Besides, she was taking a lot on herself coming to see the boy's parents. Who knew what might be the consequences if she told this perhaps explosive old man?

But the decision was taken out of her hands. Gaylord was certainly not proud of himself. In fact, he was bitterly and sincerely ashamed. But he had an unfailing eye for the dramatic, an insatiable curiosity in the reactions of adults to bizarre situations. He said, loud and clear, 'Miss Marston caught me stealing.'

The silence in the house was as heavy as on a day of lurking thunder. 'She did what?' asked Grandpa.

Miss Marston said bleakly, 'I came back to the classroom for something. Gaylord was alone. I saw him take something from David Snow's desk and put it in his pocket.'

Grandpa looked at her from under lowered brows, like a bull preparing to charge. But he said mildly, 'Some boyish joke, no doubt.'

'If you had seen his demeanour you would have known it wasn't a joke.' She was sitting with her hand protectively about Gaylord's waist. He could feel it trembling.

'What was this thing?'

'A paperweight.'

'Belonging to the school?' he asked quickly, with a sudden upthrust of his chin.

'No. One of those pretty glass ones. David had just bought it from one of the other boys.'

His gaze never left her face. 'Have you told the authorities?'

'No. I ought to have done. But I felt that there must be some explanation, some circumstance – that's why I wanted to see his parents.'

'Kind of you,' he said. 'Very kind. I wish to God you could have done.'

'Gaylord isn't a boy to steal,' she said.

One eyebrow went up. 'Can you *ever* say, Miss Marston, what another human creature will do in any given circumstances?'

'No,' she said slowly.

'No. I was afraid you might have been too young to have found that out.'

'But I still don't think Gaylord's a thief.'

Grandpa rose. 'I shall tell his parents what you say, Miss Marston. No doubt they will get in touch with you.' He shook hands. 'And thank you. Thank you for your – thoughtfulness.'

She rose and shook hands. Then she bent down and kissed Gaylord. She gave him a smile that was meant to be reassuring, but that came out anxious and nervous. Grandpa went and opened the door for her. He came back. He did not look at Gaylord. He sat down and opened the paper.

Gaylord stood and fidgeted with a bust of Milton. He had a suffocating feeling that if he didn't talk to someone soon, he would burst. But who? Great Aunt Marigold? No. He'd

111

never get it across; and if he did the shock might kill her. Gaylord was always very careful what he said to Great Aunt in case the shock killed her. Auntie Rose would be home soon. But he didn't think he wanted to tell her. She'd either recoil in horror, or clasp him to her and call him her poor lamb, neither of which he fancied. Auntie Becky would be the best to tell, he felt instinctively. She'd hear him out with that amused, friendly smile. Then she'd say, 'Well, you silly little clot. Whatever did you want to go and do that for?' And she'd give him a playful slap and go off untroubled to meet a young man.

But Becky was going straight to a dance. He'd heard her say so.

He even felt a most unusual yearning for Momma and Poppa. But Grandpa had said they wouldn't be back till the late train.

That left Grandpa.

In many ways, Gaylord had more in common with Grandpa than he had with his parents. He and Grandpa were both sturdy, independent types. They both preferred things and people to books and ideas. Gaylord looked at the old man, or at as much as he could see of him round the paper. 'Grandpa?' he said.

Grandpa peered at him round the paper. 'Do you want to make light conversation? Or do you want to discuss this blasted paperweight?'

'The paperweight,' said Gaylord miserably. 'Will they send me to prison?'

'No,' said Grandpa. 'They will not send you to prison; you can put that right out of your mind. But beyond that I can't discuss it. It's *sub judice*.'

'What's *sub judice*?'

'It means no one dares to say a damn thing about it.'

'Why not?'

Grandpa lowered his paper. 'This is a case for your parents, boy. It's their responsibility. I can't interfere in a serious matter like this. It would be both futile and improper.'

'I see,' said Gaylord, who didn't altogether, but who knew it was no use arguing with Grandpa.

The old man said, 'Find your Great Aunt. She's around somewhere. Ask her to give you something nice for your tea. Then do something you enjoy doing. Don't just hang about waiting for bedtime.'

Poppa and Momma came home flushed with triumph. They had been a great success on the Brains Trust. Momma sat in the gritty, ill-lit compartment and repeated to herself all the lugubriously witty things Poppa had said. Poppa looked at Momma, and thought how clever it was of so intelligent a woman to give a performance of such bat-witted charm. But of course that was where clever women *were* so clever. They knew that the last thing any man wanted them to be was more intelligent than himself. So they put on an act that made every male feel protective, capable, and well informed, and that went some way towards disarming even the female element.

They came home, a little above themselves. The house looked smaller and dingier than they remembered it. Not quite the place for a distinguished author and his charming, popular wife. Then they went into the living-room. And their euphoria melted.

Grandpa was up, waiting for them. And for Grandpa to be up at this time of night meant disaster. That, and the expression on Grandpa's face.

'Father,' cried Jocelyn. 'What are you doing up?' Grandpa

said, 'Sit down, both of you. I've got something to say. Oh, it's all right May. Gaylord's safe enough. It's just – '

'What?' asked Momma, feeling for a chair without taking her eyes off the old man's face.

'Miss Marston, his teacher, came to see you. She had caught Gaylord stealing from another boy's desk.'

'I don't believe it,' said Poppa at last.

'Neither do I,' said Grandpa. 'On the other hand we have the evidence of a reasonably intelligent woman, and Gaylord's own admission.'

'Gaylord admits it?'

'It was he who told me.'

Momma had sat silent, while a dozen impressions and memories tangled in her brain. Now she said, 'Willie. It's something to do with Willie.'

'It can't be, darling. Willie doesn't even go to school.'

'It is, Jocelyn. I've got a feeling. What was it he – took, father-in-law?'

'One of those glass paperweights.'

'What?'

Grandpa was surprised at the impression he had made.

'What's so peculiar about that?'

Momma said, 'Never mind, now. What happened, father-in-law? We'll have to get this straight from the beginning.'

He told them. They were silent. Then Poppa said, 'I don't care what anyone says. Gaylord's not a thief.'

Momma said, 'We must face facts, Jocelyn. On the evidence he *is* a thief. Even though he is our son.'

'Very well, then. But he was driven to it in some way.'

'Ah, I grant you that.'

Grandpa rose. 'Long past my bedtime. Good night, you two.'

May stood up and kissed him, to his obvious delight.

'Good night, father-in-law, I'm sorry you got drawn into all this.'

'Good night, my dear. Good night, Jocelyn.' He paused. 'If you want the opinion of an old man, which you probably don't – I wouldn't say Gaylord was a wrong 'un.'

'Thanks, father,' said Jocelyn. He opened the door for the old man, shut it behind him, came and took his wife's hand. 'Poor old Gaylord,' he said.

'Yes. Poor kid.' But her practical brain was already far ahead of her husband's. 'Now we can't do anything tonight, obviously. But in the morning I think he'd better stay at home and we'll try to get to the bottom of this.'

'Yes,' he said. 'Paperweight. He wanted one for Christmas. We bought him one. He wasn't interested. Now he's stolen one.'

'Willie,' she said. 'What possible connection can there be, what *possible* connection, between Willie and paper-weights?'

'I don't think there is,' he said. 'But if there is, only Gaylord can tell us what.'

They went to bed, saying they would leave it till morning. But all through the night their separate brains wrestled with the matter. Gaylord, a thief. Gaylord, their son, caught in one of the most despicable acts known to society. Long before dawn came, Momma was visiting him in Brixton, where he was serving his fifth sentence. But Poppa, with the freer imagination of the writer, had got him into the condemned cell, and the Home Secretary had just turned down a reprieve when the alarm clock sounded off.

Chapter 14

Alone among the interested parties, Gaylord had slept like a top. He awoke refreshed, and with his mind made up. He would come clean.

Momma would go on, of course. But he set against this the knowledge that what he had to say would cause considerable interest, and the altogether delightful thought that in future he would probably be taken to and from school in a police car with a flashing blue light on top. He heard his parents' alarm clock, and could hardly wait to get things off his chest.

He didn't have to wait long. In they came, in the grey morning light, smiling rather nervously, and perched one on each side of his bed. Momma looked at Poppa. Poppa took his cue, cleared his throat, and said, 'Now, old chap. What's all this we've been hearing about you?'

Gaylord said, 'It was Willie's and somebody pinched it, and Willie thought it was me only it wasn't, and Bert said he'd do me if I didn't give it back, and then Sammy Breen sold it to David Snow and so I tried to borrow it so Bert wouldn't do me.'

He paused, while Poppa tried to sort this little lot out and Momma, running absolutely true to form said, 'I thought you weren't supposed to speak to Willie. This is what comes of being deceitful, Gaylord.'

'I didn't speak to him – much.'

'Oh, no. Only enough to get yourself into a position where you had to steal something.'

'Who's Bert?' asked Poppa.

'Oh, Jocelyn! Don't be so futile. You know perfectly well. He's that hulking brother of Willie's.' Combined anxiety and relief had set Momma verging on the bloody-minded this grey morning.

'Oh, good Lord. Him,' said Poppa. 'How did he threaten you, Gaylord?'

'With a knife. He sort of dug it in here.' He indicated his soft throat. 'And he said, "If you don't give our Willie his thing back, this is going right in." ' He lay back on the pillow, well satisfied. There could be no doubt that he had captured half his audience, anyway.

But not Momma. 'Gaylord,' said Momma. 'You're sure you're not just making this up?'

Gaylord jerked upright. 'Momma. He *did*. He dug it right in here.' You would not have thought one small body could hold so much indignation.

Poppa said, 'Your mother's quite right, Gaylord. This is a very serious matter. We've got to be quite certain you're telling the truth.'

'Course I'm telling the truth.'

'There's no "of course" about it,' Momma snapped. 'You've been caught stealing and you could easily be making all this up to excuse yourself.' She looked at him gravely. 'But I don't think you are,' she said quietly.

'Course I'm not,' he said, keeping up the indignation, but thinking that perhaps Momma wasn't such a bad sort after all.

Poppa rose, and stuck his hands in his dressing-gown pockets. 'All right, old chap. We believe you. Now you'd better stay at home today, and I'll write a note to your teacher.'

Gaylord lay back once more. 'Will they send me to school in a police car?' he asked.

Momma darted him a suspicious look. But Poppa said, 'They're pretty busy, you know. I don't think they'd take on any further commitments.'

They went back to their own room. Momma shut the door carefully. Then she clutched her husband's lapels and wept as she had not wept for many, many years.

When at last she could speak: 'It's monstrous. Monstrous. A great lout like that, frightening a little boy. And with a knife.' She held him more tightly. 'Oh, Jocelyn. He might have – killed him. To think – that poor kid, going through all that, and we didn't do a thing about it.'

Poppa pressed her against his shoulder, and waited. Actually, he needed time to think. At eight in the morning his brain wasn't noted for its clarity, and he still didn't quite know what had happened. Still less did he know what he was going to do about it. So he waited patiently, hoping Momma would tell him.

He did not wait in vain. Momma lifted a tearful face and said, 'You'll have to go and see Mrs Foggerty.'

Poppa wasn't going to say, 'Who's Mrs Foggerty?' and risk having his head bitten off again. So he appeared to consider very carefully and then said, 'What about the police?'

She shook her head. 'I don't think we can, at this stage. I'm sure Gaylord's telling the truth, but – well, he could easily be exaggerating. I think you ought to see Willie's mother first.'

Well, that had established who Mrs Foggerty was, anyway. Not that Poppa relished the idea of visiting the lady, especially since Momma didn't sound as though she was coming. Still, he wasn't one to evade his responsibilities. Two hours later he set off for the Foggerty household.

Someone had stuck a row of dejected, urban-looking houses in a country lane, and it was in one of these that the Foggerties lived. Poppa knocked with a show of confidence he did not feel. Mrs Foggerty opened, and looked at him with the utmost suspicion. Then, deciding he wasn't after either the rent, the insurance, or the telly, she gripped her fag more tightly between her lips and said, 'Come on in.'

'Thank you,' said Poppa, taking off his hat and stepping inside.

Mrs Foggerty watched this little performance with a surprise and approval she made no attempt to disguise. She wasn't used to men who took off their hats and said thank you. 'You're Mr Pentecost, aren't you?' she said. 'I've heard your things on the wireless.'

'Indeed?' Poppa looked gratified.

The necessity for keeping a grip on her cigarette gave a somewhat slurred quality to Mrs Foggerty's speech, rather like that of a third-rate ventriloquist. 'I reckon it's clever, being able to write.'

Poppa looked even more gratified. A pity some of the family didn't realize this. 'I don't know how you think of things,' said Mrs Foggerty.

'No? Well –' said Poppa. But he had not come to discuss the springs of the creative impulse, much as he would have preferred to. 'I believe you have a son, Bert,' he said.

'That's him,' said Mrs Foggerty, and for the first time Jocelyn began to take in his surroundings, a confused welter, of which the most obvious feature was the smell of wet washing, stew and paraffin; and in which the human interest was supplied by a youth sitting in shirt-sleeves and braces at the kitchen table. Bert had an old copy of the *Mirror* open on the table and was searching it, apparently without success, for something of interest.

'My little boy says that Bert threatened him with a knife,' said Jocelyn.

'Here! Bert!' Mrs Foggerty claimed her son's attention by kicking him sharply on the ankle. 'Did you threaten Mr Pentecost's little boy with a knife?'

Bert looked up. 'No,' he said. He went on with his reading.

Mrs Foggerty came back to her visitor. 'There,' she said. 'See?' She had done her bit. The matter was closed.

It was very difficult. Never in his life had Jocelyn called anyone a liar. He said, choosing his words carefully, 'But my son says he did. And naturally I believe my own son.'

'So do I, cock,' said Mrs Foggerty, lighting a cigarette from the stub of the old one.

Jocelyn let this pass. He said, 'Your son accused Gaylord of stealing Willie's paperweight. Then he held a knife against his throat and said he'd drive it in if he didn't give it back.'

'Yes, but I mean. It's just your kid's word against my Bert's, isn't it?' The cigarette smoke drifted up her face, teasing her nostrils and her eyes. 'I mean, your kid could be telling lies, couldn't he?'

'He could. But he isn't.'

'Oh, well.' She shrugged. 'If you're going to take that attitude.' She spoke in sorrow much more than in anger. 'My kid's been to Borstal and yours is going to Eton, I suppose, so yours must be right. You're using your class, Mr Pentecost.'

'Look. Where's Willie? Ask him whether he ever had a paperweight.'

'No good asking him. He'd never remember.' She looked at Jocelyn sadly, 'Mr Pentecost, haven't you anything better to do than come badgering a widow who's doing her best to keep a home together and look after a softie?'

Poppa had never felt such a heel in his life. All he wanted to do now was apologize for his behaviour, give the poor soul five shillings to keep the home together, and run for it.

And then, suddenly, he thought of Gaylord, carrying, until this morning, his lonely burden of fear. He remembered his wife's tears. He saw, in a blinding flash of awareness, the violence, the sour, joyless violence that in his lifetime had turned the sweet world into a vast, man-made hell for millions. And this – this business was the whole thing in microcosm. If he held his peace now he deserved to go down himself into the hell. He marched back into the room, and banged both fists down on the table. 'Listen, you,' he said.

He found himself looking into eyes whose inhumanity terrified him. There was a gulf here that no one – priest, doctor, executioner – no one could cross. Neither love nor friendship nor hate nor retribution would ever wring any response from those eyes. Jocelyn said, 'You threatened my boy. And now I'm warning you. If you ever go near him again I'll have the police down on you like – like a ton of bricks.'

His voice had been shaking. He was breathing heavily. There were tears of rage in his eyes. And the one thing he hated above all others was to lose control. But he still leaned over the table, his clenched fists pressed against the woodwork. And still those expressionless eyes stared into his. Then the pale, unhealthy lips twisted. 'Aw, get stuffed,' said Bert Foggerty, and went back to his study of last week's news.

Jocelyn straightened up. 'I've warned you,' he said. 'I mean it.' He stood for a few moments, regaining control. Then he went to the door. Mrs Foggerty opened it for him.

Bygones apparently were bygones. 'You ever get anything on telly, Mr Pentecost?' she asked chattily.

'No.'

'Well, perhaps you will one day if you keep trying,' she said encouragingly. 'You get a lot on the wireless, don't you.'

He came home. Momma said, 'I've learnt something else while you've been away. You remember how ill Gaylord looked on Christmas Day? Well, one of those Foggerty louts had been twisting his arm.'

Poppa stared at her. 'Oh, my God,' he said. He was one of those who believe there should be a special hell reserved for people who twist a little boy's arm.

She looked at him in alarm. 'Darling, I've never seen you look so angry.'

'I've never been so angry. An oaf like that, daring to touch Gaylord.' He was still quivering.

'Look,' she said. 'There's only one thing for you to do. Go for a ten-mile walk and get it out of your system. Then you can sit down quietly and tell me all about Mrs Foggerty.'

'Yes,' he said. 'Yes. Bless you, May.' He set off, slashing with his stick at the wet, grey grass. Dear May! How had he thought of her in that perceptive moment on Christmas morning? Wife, mother, friend, mistress? Well, today she was mother, sending her angry child off alone to make his own peace with his own soul. But how, he wondered, does she know so unfailingly which role I need her to put on at any moment. How can she see so clearly into my very heart?

But he was still obsessed with thoughts of pain and violence and cruelty. A bully twisting a boy's arm, Auschwitz, Sharpeville; they were all part of the same thing, they differed only in degree. He strode on, seeking an answer where there was no answer. And yet, as he went on, the rhythm of his walking, and the rough, friendly road under his shoes, and the grey, still, dead winter's day all brought their own comfort. So that when he came home he had found no answers, but he had found a certain peace within himself, and he knew he could not hope for more.

He had also decided that, for the time being at any rate, Gaylord must not go beyond the garden alone. He, Jocelyn, would take him to school and bring him back. He and May would take the boy for picnics when the weather improved. But Gaylord must not go alone. It was a damnable thing; but a menace now hung over this quiet, pastoral countryside. Violence walked in the lanes, lurked in the meadows. And though, taking the sensible view, it did not seem likely that an adolescent like Bert would carry on a vendetta against a small boy, it was not a matter on which you could afford to take any risks.

Chapter 15

Spring came bleak, with the lambs shivering like small boys watching a football match, and the daffodils naked to the east wind, and the river cold and grey as Lethe, and the protesting rooks flung helplessly about the sky. Then, suddenly, everything was different. The air was soft, and a quiet benevolence lay on the countryside. The boles of trees were varnished with sunlight. The river sparkled. The sky was alive with many-coloured clouds.

And that was only the beginning. The silver birches put on their frocks of tender green, the blackthorn scattered its snow-flurries on the grass, the dramatic skies of April towered over the land. And May and Jocelyn walked together in wonder, and cried as they cried every year, 'Surely no other spring was ever quite so lovely.'

For Rose, at any rate, this was certainly true. Rose, for the first time in her life, was experiencing the joy of requited love. Bobs, after a slow start, had become quite attentive. True, Rose didn't often get him to herself. But, together with Becky and Peter, they made up a fairly satisfactory quartet. They played tennis, they went for long drives in the still evenings, they ate cosy, candle-lit dinners in country inns. And sometimes, on these happy occasions, Bobs would hold her hand and even kiss her with every appearance of enjoyment. Oh, it was wonderful, and Rose burgeoned with the burgeoning countryside, living for the minute, knowing in her heart that this was something that could not last, that she had the word 'spinster' stamped all over her. And, in her woman's heart, she knew other things. She knew Bobs didn't really love her, and that anyway he wasn't the marrying kind. She knew it wasn't going to last, and she didn't think she wanted it to. But it was her last chance. She would gather what few, late roses she could, before the frosts came.

Gaylord was also enjoying the spring. Sometimes he and Grandpa would stump together round the farm, Gaylord's small hand encased in the old man's great horny fist. Sometimes he would wander with Momma and Poppa, wading knee-deep in a lake of bluebells or gazing, with the long thoughts of childhood, at the murmuring river.

Now, though he would never have admitted it, he was rather relieved to have an escort wherever he went. It gave him a sense of importance, even though his parents tried to make it seem as casual as possible. But more than that he really was scared of the young Foggerties. They were a gang of dangerous, destructive kids, with as many chips as shoulders; but seen from Gaylord's eye level they were all seven feet high and ruthless killers. He knew that if he met them alone he would be outnumbered, outpaced, and outfought, and the suffering he had known at the hands of Willie would be multiplied a thousand fold. Which didn't even bear thinking of.

But there was one fly in his ointment. His fondness for the normally gentle and simple Willie went very deep, and it worried him that he no longer saw his friend. Besides, he forgot the pain of his twisted arm, and remembered only Willie's almost animal distress when he lost his bauble. Willie was now his favourite cause. In some vague way he wanted to make up to Willie for the fact that he was only ninepence to the shilling and lived in a miserable house, and wore jumble sale clothes. And the only way he knew would be to sit in the old quarry and listen to Willie's silences. It wasn't much. But at least it was more than anyone else seemed prepared to do.

And, in the old quarry the brambles pushed forth their long strands; and the bracken that had begun life as a thousand shepherd's crooks, tiny and tender and green, the bracken was knee high. Everything was thrusting and shoving and jostling in the annual summer rush for a place in the sun. Summer! And one that so far was not being bloody-minded. The deckchairs were out in the orchard. Poppa sat writing with the sun warm on his cheek. Gaylord sprawled on the grass, drawing. Momma sat in the shade, indolent, content, feeling the new life stirring in her body, knowing herself at one with the teeming, fruitful earth. She too would have her harvest home. The laughter lines deepened round her closed eyes. Poppa, who was watching her, said, 'A penny for them, May.'

She opened her eyes, gave him a smile of lazy affection. 'I was thinking Gaylord II should be here in time for the harvest festival.'

'Oh.' He looked disappointed. 'I thought it would be funnier than that.'

'The Vicar might like him to decorate the font with. After all, he'll be part of the Parish harvest.' She chuckled happily. Poppa looked lost. 'Never mind,' she said. 'Gaylord II thought it was funny, anyway.' She closed her eyes, and floated to and fro between sleep and waking like a piece of driftwood at the sea's edge. Jocelyn, too, was thinking better with his eyes shut. Gaylord wriggled away silently on his stomach, like a Red Indian or a serpent.

Then, having made his escape, he paused. He wanted to see his friend; but he certainly didn't want to see his friend's brothers. So he went very carefully. And when he came to the old quarry, he stopped and listened with a beating heart.

Only the grasshoppers, the twitter of gossiping sparrows, the ubiquitous bees. He worked his way inside very quietly, and was rewarded by finding Willie alone. He blew out his cheeks with relief.

It was nice to come into the tangle of the old quarry, and be greeted by Willie's smile. Willie's smile was as warm and beneficent as the sunshine. 'Hello, Gaylord,' he said. 'Thought you'd gone away or something.'

'No. Been busy,' said Gaylord, idly digging a hole in the sandy soil.

The sun was hot. The quarry smelt of warm sand, and rock, and foxgloves, and bracken. Gaylord squinted up in the brilliance at Willie, and smiled. He was glad Willie was his old self again, everything forgotten. The afternoon crept on. They said little. But they were content, being together, enjoying the long silences. At last Willie said, 'You know our Bert?'

Gaylord's inside lurched. He nodded.

'He's going to do you,' said Willie.

Gaylord concentrated on his digging. 'Why?' he asked.

'You was rude. And your dad was rude.' Willie sounded reproving.

Gaylord wished more than ever that he hadn't cocked that snook. He went on digging.

'You know our Dave?' said Willie.

'Yes,' said Gaylord unhappily.

'He's going to do you, too. You was rude. And your dad was.'

The shadows were deep, now, in the quarry. 'You know our Mike?' said Willie.

It was no good. The glory had departed. Gaylord stood up. 'I've got to go now, Willie,' he said, wishing to goodness he hadn't come in the first place.

Willie looked disappointed. 'You don't never come now, Gaylord. And when you do you don't stop.'

Gaylord dusted the sand from his shorts. 'My father's never rude,' he said.

'Our Arthur says he was,' said Willie. 'He's going to do you for it.'

Becky, on the grass, was nut-brown all over, except presumably for the few square inches covered by her sun-suit. Rose, whose only response to the sun was to turn dull and mottled, sat talking to Bobs in the shade. Bobs listened to Rose and looked at Becky. Peter looked at Becky. Aunt Marigold and Grandpa looked at Becky. And Aunt Marigold thought, you didn't see that sort of thing in my young days, and Grandpa thought the same and added, more's the pity, dammit. So they sat, or lay, or sprawled, content, while the sun crept, with commendable slowness, down the cloudless sky. Only the bees were working, the poor suckers, and the sound of their labours was just what idle man needed to lull and drowse him into sleep.

It was an afternoon of rare content. One of those days when the warmth of the sun seeps even into the heart. Bobs said quietly to Rose, 'What about a run on Sunday? We could take a picnic tea, if you like. Have it on the Beacon.'

She could hardly believe her ears. 'You mean – just the two of us?'

'Yes. What about it?'

'Bobs, I'd love to. What time will you call for me?'

'Two-thirty?'

'Yes. I'll be ready.'

I bet you will, he thought, wishing she'd make the chase a bit more worth while. Poor old Rose. Falling over backwards in her efforts to please. It took all the excitement out of things.

But now at last the sun was westering. A little breeze flurried the orchard leaves. High overhead two birds flew homeward. 'Let's call it a day,' the bees said, and went back to the hive. The humans rose, yawned, shivered. Drugged and drowsed with sunlight they trailed indoors, pulling their deck-chairs behind them. Only Poppa looked behind. Nothing left now of the long peace of that summer's afternoon; nothing but a few imprints on the grass, and a book lying open under the trees, and the evening star, growing more golden every minute, come to bring home all that the bright day had scattered...

All? All? Where in God's name was Gaylord, thought Poppa as he came into the house. He had a confused idea that he had been with them all afternoon. Yet he hadn't seen him when they began to trek. He hurried back to the orchard.

Gaylord was so absorbed in his drawing that he didn't notice Poppa until he spoke. Poppa said, 'You – you've not been there all the time, have you?'

Gaylord's look of astonishment made Poppa feel half-witted. 'I've been *drawing*,' said Gaylord.

'Oh,' said Poppa, looking helpless. 'Well, you'd better come in. It's turning chilly.' He followed Gaylord thoughtfully into the house. Really, he *must* try not to be so absent-minded. Not even noticing his own son...

Chapter 16

Rose thought Sunday would never come. But it did, and by breakfast-time the sun had gathered warmth, the birds were singing, the bees were buzzing, the hens were contentedly clucking, the smoke was standing up blue and straight from cottage chimneys. Oh, it was a perfect, exquisite morning; there was joy in the tiny, hurrying spider, in the fat, metal-hued fly; there was joy in the fish, lying cool and still against the stream; in the dappled, sun-dappled cattle ambling down the lane to their milking; joy in the worm upthrusting and the sun down-pouring; joy in earth and surely joy in heaven at such a satisfactory creation; joy most of all perhaps in the heart of Rose, who was going to spend the afternoon alone with her love.

Suppose she had been wrong about him. Suppose he did ask her to marry him! Yes, that *was* what she wanted, really. Still, even if he didn't, they would be alone, together, on the high, lonely Beacon, caught between earth and heaven, with only the larks and sky above them, and the world of men crawling like ants far, far below. They would be alone. It was a thought almost unbearable in its promise of joy.

Instead of slipping in to breakfast in her usual mousy fashion. Rose made quite an entrance. 'What a lovely, lovely morning,' she cried.

'Thunder in the air,' said Grandpa, not lifting his eyes from the *Observer.*

Rose's heart plummeted. But Gaylord's soared. 'Do you think we shall have a storm. Grandpa?'

'Be surprised if we don't.'

Gaylord's eyes shone. Of all the things that happened in his young life, thunderstorms were perhaps the nicest. There was all the noise you could want; and no one, so far, not even Momma, had tried to blame him for it. They were free; you didn't have to decide whether to have a thunderstorm or a quarter of bull's-eyes. And they terrified the women. Even Momma lost a bit of her bounce when it thundered.

But Grandpa's words had depressed Rose unutterably. She knew from experience that Bobs wasn't one to trifle with the elements. You wouldn't get Bobs up the Beacon in a thunderstorm. She had a quite unreasonable feeling that today was critical. Let them go on this picnic alone together, and well – anything might happen. But let it be spoilt, then it would be the end of the affair. The thing would fizzle out, die of inaction and lost opportunity. Why she felt like this she did not know. Sheer imagination, of course. She must be run down. End of term blues, she would have thought, if there hadn't been another two months to go yet.

As soon as breakfast was over she ran up to her room and looked out of the window. Still the same, lovely morning. Father must be wrong. He was just putting on a weather-wise yokel act.

No, she had to admit, father was too genuine to put on acts. (Except his 'I'm just an old man, they never tell me anything' one, which fooled nobody.) And there *was* a white bank of cloud very low on the eastern horizon. She went and tapped the barometer. It sank, and she was ready to weep with disappointment and self-pity. If, after such a lovely week, it rained now, she would take it as a personal affront.

But she would not think about rain. She would concentrate all her energies and thoughts on preparing the picnic.

In the kitchen she nearly drove Momma, who was cooking Sunday dinner, mad. Wherever Momma turned there was Rose, slicing cucumber, spreading *pâté de foie gras*, reducing tomatoes to a pulpy, bloody mess. And there was Great Aunt Marigold, doing nothing in particular and doing it, unlike the House of Peers, not very well. And there was Becky, looking at Rose's wafer-thin sandwiches and saying, 'Darling, those aren't for a man, are they?'

'Yes,' said Rose, slicing and flushing angrily.

'But darling, he'll pop three of those in at once and not know he'd had them. Like a great big whale swallowing plankton.'

'Will you mind your own bloody business,' cried Rose.

'Hoity toity,' said Great Aunt Marigold.

'I'm only trying to be helpful, dear. A man's idea of a sandwich is a couple of doorsteps with two ounces of butter and a quarter of ham in the middle.'

It is a law of nature that no kitchen, however large, is big enough to hold two women, let alone four. And whatever the weather outside, there was already more than a touch of thunder in the kitchen. Momma, who was having her own little disagreements with Gaylord II this morning said, 'I wish you'd stop bickering, you two.'

'We are not bickering,' said Rose. 'Becky is just being her usual interfering, infuriating self.'

'Dear sister.' Becky smiled indulgently.

Gaylord came in. 'Can I have a sandwich, Auntie Rose?'

'No,' said Rose.

'But I'm famished.'

Rose said nothing. 'They don't look very big,' said Gaylord. 'What's that grey stuff?'

'*Pâté de foie gras*,' said Becky.

'It smells awful,' said Gaylord.

'Nobody asked your opinion,' said Rose.

Momma took command. 'Stop being a nuisance, Gaylord. Come on, out you go. I won't have you indoors on a lovely morning like this.'

'It isn't a lovely morning. It's gone all cloudy and horrid.'

Rose dropped what she was doing and ran to the window. Gaylord was right. The sun, that had smiled down so joyously, was now filmed and troubled, like a dying goldfish.

Momma looked at Gaylord. 'Out,' she said, with that unrelenting persistence that, he thought, was one of her most unattractive traits. He went; his thin, departing shoulders registering hunger, disapproval and lack of affection. 'I wish we'd thought to give him a sandwich,' said Aunt Marigold brightly. 'His father was always one for a sandwich when he was his age.'

'He still is,' said Momma, adding ruefully to herself, I bet Gaylord II could do with one, too, the way he's carrying on.

Midday dinner was over, and cleared away. Rose looked out at the lowering landscape. If only it would hold off until after two-thirty. If only they could at least get away in the car, before the heavens fell.

As fall they were certainly going to. For some time now the thunder had been growling and snarling in the distance, building up tension in the room as only thunder can. Gaylord's stomach was fluttering like a trapped bird. His brown knees quaked. He responded as the hushed and waiting earth responded. But he loved it. He strolled across and joined his grandfather at the window. He stuck his hands in the pockets of his shorts. This was an occasion when the men were in command of the situation, an occasion to be made the most of. 'I can't understand *anyone* being afraid of thunder,' he observed chattily.

'No?' said Grandpa.

'*I* shouldn't be afraid if it struck the house,' said Gaylord. He looked at Great Aunt Marigold, whose old fingers were fumbling at the aspirin bottle. He looked at Auntie Rose, whose eyes kept straying apprehensively to the window.

'Where's Becky?' asked Aunt Marigold.

'In her room. Tarting herself up,' said Rose bitterly.

'She oughtn't to go out –' began Great Aunt. But at this moment Becky came into the room. She was wearing a billowy sort of frock and a great cartwheel of a hat. She was showing her white teeth in a brilliant smile. Gaylord looked at her with approval. But Grandpa said, sourly. 'If you're going out you'd be better in gum boots and a mackintosh.'

'I shouldn't look so nice.'

'You'd look a damn sight more sensible,' snapped Rose.

The two sisters looked at each other. 'Darling,' cooed Becky, 'the last thing any man wants a girl to look is sensible.'

Grandpa looked at his daughters with irritation, wondering vaguely how he could have helped to produce two such opposites. He wished they'd get themselves married. With Becky, of course, it was only a matter of time. But Rose? Despite her sallowness, he thought, her face had a certain sculptural beauty. But it wouldn't last. In a year or two, men would think her features heavy. Then where would she be? He sighed. Why didn't she grab this Roberts feller before it was too late?

The two silly bitches were still staring at each other. Just like a couple of alley cats. Grandpa could stand it no longer. 'Why the hell don't you go if you're going?' he shouted.

Becky swept him a curtsy, and went, still smiling. She left behind a fragrance of scent and fresh linen.

'Going to meet a fellow, by the look of things,' said Great Aunt Marigold, delighted by her own perspicacity.

Momma came briskly in from the kitchen. 'Gaylord, come away from that window. It's thundering.'

Wasn't that typical? Just because he enjoyed thunderstorms he couldn't watch them. 'Grandpa's standing by the window,' he pointed out.

'When you're as old as Grandpa you can do as you like. In the meantime – '

Gaylord sighed. Momma always had an answer that satisfied her, even if it satisfied no one else. But now she had turned her attention to Rose. 'Hasn't that young man of yours turned up yet. Rose?'

'Does it look like it?' said Rose.

Momma, thanks to Gaylord II and the thunder, was in no mood to be snapped at. 'He's not very ardent, dear,' she said.

Rose did not reply. She dropped her eyes to her magazine. But all she saw was a blur. Bobs hadn't come, and now even May, sweet, sunny, equable May, had turned bitchy. It was the last little straw. She sat with lowered head, and a tear fell on to her book, like the first, slow, heavy drop of the coming storm.

But the room was already too dark, too vibrant with electricity, for anyone to notice. Gaylord was as fizzy as a glass of health salts. Well, if he couldn't watch from the window, he decided, he would do his disappearing act. Casually he wandered into the kitchen. Very quietly he opened the back door. Then he was outside, under the leaden sky.

You could almost feel the weight of clouds on your shoulders. They surged, they billowed, black and dirty. There was a muted twittering from the birds, crouched in the hedgerows like children in church, awed, fidgety, waiting for the service to begin. The cattle had ceased their grazing. They stood, solid, ruminant, yet on the edge of panic. The river gleamed dully, like molten lead. Distance had an unusual clarity, as though seen through field-glasses. Everything – the trees, the church spire, the far hills – had shifted a little nearer. The landscape was closing in, infinitely menacing.

Gaylord shivered deliciously. And made his plans. This was something he *wasn't* going to watch with mother. She'd be putting her hands over his eyes every time it lightened. Using every bit of cover he ran for the barn. And reached its dark interior unobserved.

The barn smelt of potatoes, and hay, and firewood; and the earthy, dusty smell of the stored centuries. It was a place of infinite delights. When Gaylord grew up he was going to live here, sleeping in the sweet hay and eating off the old chopping-block. But now he clambered up the ladder to the loft, wriggled like a snake across the hay, and lay with his bright eyes peering out of the doorway that opened so excitingly on to nothingness. From here he could see the whole thunder-haunted valley, the meanders of the river, and the far, black, turgid heart of the storm.

Suddenly, far away, a jag of lightning leapt through the belly of a cloud, and pierced the earth. It was like a signal for the show to begin. The thunder was suddenly overhead, banging and rattling around the sky, dying away, coming louder, finally wandering away among the hills. But now there was more lightning, brighter, nearer, close at hand. It was like needles darting at your eyes. And the thunder was so close it was even inside your own head. Despite his boasting Gaylord was scared. Not that he would have admitted it, even to himself. And when he suddenly realized he was going to have company he used the most terrible oath. 'Hell and damn,' said Gaylord, when he saw Auntie Becky running towards the barn hand in hand with Auntie Rose's lover.

He heard them coming up the ladder, whispering and laughing. He burrowed into the hay, trying not to breathe. He didn't trust grown-ups, not any of them. And he didn't much like Auntie Rose's lover. He thought him foolish. He showed all his teeth when he laughed, which made him look like a horse. And Gaylord was a little puzzled as to why he was with Auntie Becky. But he had long since given up expecting grown-ups to behave in a predictable manner. They never failed to surprise you. And, anyway, he was too interested in the storm to give the matter much thought.

A few drops of rain were falling, now; plopping down as fat and heavy as toads. He heard Auntie Becky's voice, somewhere near at hand. 'It's starting,' she panted. 'We were only just in time.'

'Shouldn't have liked you to get that nice frock wet,' said Auntie Rose's lover. 'You look too damn pretty in it.'

'Do I, Bobs?' And Gaylord imagined the quick smile with which she would say it. 'I think Rose has got one of her sick headaches,' she went on.

'Poor Rose,' said Bobs.

'Yes. Poor Rose.' Auntie Becky giggled. Then they were silent.

It was raining with a vengeance, now. Drumming on the roof, making streams and runnels in the stack yard, pocking the smooth surface of the river. And the thunder roared and shouted, and the lightning glinted on wet grass and in a thousand puddles. Auntie Becky said, caressingly, 'It looks as though we're going to be here some time, Bobs.'

Auntie Rose's young man did not reply. But then, after a few seconds, he kissed Auntie Becky. And went on kissing her. Gaylord heard him, and felt again his vague sense of surprise. Not that he blamed the young man. Although Gaylord was definitely not the kissing type, he quite liked kissing Auntie Becky himself.

But the storm had passed its best, now. It was trundling away to the east, leaving only a steady rain. Gaylord was suddenly bored. He'd seen all he wanted to see. Now he was prepared to be sociable. He rose from the hay like Neptune from the waves, and wandered amiably over for a chat with Auntie Becky and Auntie Rose's lover.

But even Gaylord sensed that he wasn't welcome. Auntie Becky's face was very pink. Her eyes were scared. 'Gaylord! How long have you been here?' she asked.

'Ages and ages,' he said. 'I was nearly struck once. I felt it run all down my arm.'

Auntie Becky was watching him closely. 'Did you know Mr Roberts and I were here?'

'Yes, of course. I heard you come up.'

'We were caught in the storm,' Auntie Becky said. 'We had to shelter.' Her big hat lay in the hay beside her. She pulled it towards her, began playing with the ribbons.

'Yes, I know,' Gaylord said, rather shortly. He might be very young, but they didn't have to explain things to him quite so thoroughly. He moved towards the ladder. 'Where are you going?' demanded Auntie Becky.

138

'Back to the house,' he said. He addressed himself to Mr Roberts. 'I'll tell Auntie Rose you're here,' he said kindly. 'She thought you weren't coming.'

'No,' Mr Roberts said quickly. 'No. You needn't do that, Gaylord.' He fumbled in his pocket. 'Here. Do you like sweets?' He gave Gaylord a shilling.

'Thanks, Mr Roberts,' Gaylord said politely. He went and grasped the top of the ladder.

'Gaylord,' his aunt called.

He paused. 'Yes, Auntie Becky?'

'Oh, nothing,' she said. Gaylord went on down. He was beginning to wonder whether Auntie Becky was a bit barmy.

He ran across the stack yard, cold rain on his head, cold puddles splashing round his knees. He reached the warm gloom of the living-room. 'Gaylord, where have you been?' cried Momma.

'Watching the storm,' he said. 'From a Secret Place.'

'Well, you'd no business,' Grandpa said testily. 'Your mother's been worried to death.' He banged his chair arm with his fist. 'I don't know. Women! Your Great Aunt's been having the vapours because of a bit of thunder, and Rose here moping and mowing because her young man hasn't turned up –'

Gaylord was pleased to be the bearer of glad tidings. 'Oh, *he's* all right. He's in the hay loft with Auntie Becky,' he said reassuringly.

The reception of this piece of good news quite startled Gaylord. Slowly his aunt straightened up from her chair. 'What did you say?' she demanded. Her rather muddy features had turned white. She seemed to Gaylord to be towering higher and higher over him. '*What* did you say?'

'I said he was all right. I thought you might think he'd been struck by lightning, or something.'

'I wish he had been,' said Auntie Rose bitterly.

'*I* was – nearly,' Gaylord said. He grimaced, rubbed his arm. 'I felt it, all up there. All tingly.' But Auntie Rose was unimpressed. In fact, she didn't seem to be listening. Not to Gaylord, anyway. She was listening to footsteps – brisk, clattering footsteps that were coming across the kitchen. Then the door opened, and Auntie Becky came in. Gay, poised, demure as ever – but with straw in her straw-coloured hair.

Auntie Rose strode across to her. 'Where is he?'

Becky looked at her with a pretty, puzzled frown. 'Who, darling?'

'You know who. Bobs, of course.'

'Dearest, how should I know? Hasn't he come to see you?'

'No, he hasn't. And shall I tell you why? Because you waylaid him.'

'But what nonsense. I haven't even seen him.' All this was a revelation to Gaylord. They'd always given him the impression that *he* was the only one who told lies; that grown-ups were incapable of an untruth. And here was Auntie Becky telling whoppers with a fluency he could not but admire.

But Auntie Rose had groped her way to the table, and lowered herself into a chair, stiffly, like an old woman. She sounded dreadfully weary. 'Damn you, Becky,' she said. 'You've had every man who's ever come near the place. Only one of them has ever looked at me. Bobs. The only one. And now you've got him, too. Damn you, Becky.'

Becky flounced towards the stairs. 'I don't know what you're talking about,' she said.

And then Mr Roberts came into the room. 'Sorry I'm late. Rose,' he began. 'The storm – '

But he got no farther. Rose stared at him as though hypnotized. Still staring, she rose, while her hands groped about the table. Her fingers closed on a pair of scissors – and suddenly she flung herself at Bobs.

'No,' he cried. 'No,' twisting away, and the point of the scissors tore a great gash in his sleeve. For a moment Rose went on staring at him, mouth and eyes wide open. Then she dropped the scissors, and fell into a chair, weeping hysterically.

Gaylord was watching, fascinated. This last bit was, if anything, even more satisfactory than the storm.

And it had been a bit like the storm. Everybody had been quiet, sort of frozen. And then – suddenly, everything had happened at once, with the scissors flashing and Grandpa shouting to Rose not to be a damn fool, and the women all screaming and Mr Roberts yelling his head off. And then, right at the end, just the rain – Rose's tears.

Gaylord watched her weeping with cool detachment. Her face had gone all blotchy, and she was making dreadful groaning noises in her throat. And there was in her face a drained look of hopelessness, as though she wanted to die and couldn't. Gaylord decided he would never marry Auntie Rose. She looked messy. Besides, he felt, after today's exhibition you could never, ever trust her.

Then Momma, with her perfect genius for spoiling things, got hold of him and dragged him from the room. Still, he was not dissatisfied. He'd had a lovely day. He'd seen a storm, and he had nearly been struck by lightning. He'd heard Auntie Becky telling whoppers, and he'd seen Auntie Rose going potty with the scissors. Grown-ups, he decided, weren't always quite as perfect as they tried to make out.

Today he had learnt one or two things that might come in useful, next time they accused him of anything.

Only two men had ever shown any interest in Rose – Bobs, and Stan Grebbie. Only two men had ever made her heart beat faster. And one of them was far away, teaching in County Durham. She wasn't likely to see him again. And the other had done this to her.

She lay face downwards on her bed, still weeping convulsively. There was a knock at the door. 'Go away,' cried Rose.

The door opened. May came in, sat down on the bed, and took her sister-in-law in her arms. 'Don't, Rose. Don't,' she pleaded.

'Go away,' said Rose, trying to throw herself back on to the bed.

May hung on firmly: 'Rose, dear, don't. He's not worth it. There's not a man alive worth it.' Except one, she added to herself.

'Where is he?'

'Gone. He took one look at your father's face and ran for his life.'

Rose was a little less violent, now. 'I never want to see him again – as long as I live.'

May held the poor, blubbering head against her breast. 'I can't say I blame you. You're worth someone better, my dear.'

'No I'm not. I'm the most unattractive creature alive.'

'Don't talk such nonsense,' May said sharply. Rose's tears began again. Oh God, thought May. How can one give comfort where there is no comfort? She held Rose more tightly. 'Why don't you get your things off and pop into bed, and I'll bring you a nice cup of tea?'

'Tea! That's all anyone can ever think of in a crisis.'

That's because it's all there is left, thought May. The bottom drops out of the world, and the only thing left is to drink a cup of tea and then start the long climb out of the pit. 'Rose, dear,' she said with great tenderness. 'You've got to pull yourself together.'

'Why?' said Rose. She was sitting up on the bed now. Her drooping shoulders looked as though they would never again support the world. The door opened. Becky came in.

Rose stared at her. May said coldly, 'What are you doing here, Becky?'

Becky said, 'I want to talk to Rose. Alone.'

'Get out,' said Rose.

'Leave it till later, for God's sake,' said May.

'I want to speak to her now.' This was a new Becky, commanding and stern. For a long moment she and May looked at each other. Then May went out and shut the door behind her.

'Get out,' Rose said again. She was sitting now with her head lolling against the bed head, staring at her sister with hatred, contempt, and an infinite weariness.

Becky said, 'I was off to meet Peter. But I ran into Bobs just as the rain started. We *had* to shelter.'

Rose went on staring at her in silence. Becky said, 'It wasn't anything planned. What happened was just chance and – I suppose two rather worthless characters.'

Rose went on staring. 'Have you finished?' she said at last.

'I would like to ask your forgiveness. Not now, but some time.'

The wide-eyed stare slowly, very slowly, detached itself from Becky's face and swung to the window. After a time Becky turned and left the room. Rose did not appear to see her go.

Chapter 17

'A bit of slap and tickle in the hayloft is one thing. Causing riot and civil commotion is another.' Grandpa had got his fighting boots on.

Becky had got hers on, too. 'It *wasn't* slap and tickle. Don't be so earthy. Father. I let him kiss me, which he enjoyed, and which I enjoyed – '

'And which Rose enjoyed hearing about, I don't doubt,' said May.

'You keep out of this,' they both told her.

'I'm hanged if I'll keep out of it. I think Rose has been treated abominably.'

Grandpa hated having a third party intervene in a really good row. It dispersed his fire-power. 'Be quiet, May,' he snapped.

'Anyway,' said Becky. 'How *did* Rose hear about it? From Gaylord.'

'Oh, I see. So it was all Gaylord's fault, I suppose.'

The debate continued. Poppa, who had been walking doggedly for most of the day, and sheltering in a barn for part of it, wrestling with a recalcitrant plot. Poppa came home, his mind full now of thoughts of supper, slippers, and a quiet pipe. But as soon as he entered the living-room he knew that these things were not for him. Father was pacing the quarter deck, about to clap the entire crew in irons. Poppa's heart sank. 'Is something the matter?' he asked.

Grandpa turned on him. 'And where have you been, just when you were needed?'

'Walking,' said Poppa. 'And thinking,' he added in extenuation.

Grandpa did not hide his contempt for this statement. 'Well, what's happened?' asked Poppa.

'I'll tell you what's happened. Becky here seduced Rose's young man in the hayloft.'

'Oh, is that all?' said Poppa, disappointed. If they'd had a family scene every time Becky took a young man into the hayloft, he thought, well –

'No it isn't all. Not by a long chalk. Afterwards Rose went for this fellow Roberts with a pair of scissors.'

'With a pair of scissors?' Poppa was horrified.

'Yes, dammit. Might have killed the poor little bastard.'

May said thoughtfully, 'For a retired solicitor, your choice of words is often surprising.'

Grandpa glared. 'Don't you criticize my choice of words, young woman.'

'Don't speak to May like that,' said Poppa.

'I didn't seduce him,' said Becky.

'You surprise me,' said Poppa.

'Well, what a horrible thing to say to your own sister,' said Momma.

Poppa began to feel a little dizzy. He didn't seem able to work out who was on whose side. 'If you ask me,' he said, 'the sooner Becky gets herself married the better it will be for all concerned.'

The old man stared at him in amazement. Then: 'Good Lord, Jocelyn. You've made a sensible remark for once. Becky! This fellow of yours. Will he marry you, do you think?'

'I don't happen to have asked him,' Becky said coldly.

'Well, it's time you did. The sooner you're out of this house the better, before Rose does you bodily harm or I have a nervous breakdown. And if you don't ask him, I will.'

Grandpa and Becky were now facing each other across the table. Becky struck it with her clenched fist. 'How dare you threaten me with a shotgun wedding?'

'Call it a shotgun wedding if you like,' said her father. 'But you're going to marry that young man before it's too late.'

Gaylord, passing the door on a foraging expedition, gave his pyjamas a hitch and wondered what a shotgun wedding was. Perhaps, he thought, it was like a wedding he went to once where they had an arch of swords; only with an arch of shotguns instead of swords. It sounded nice, especially if they all fired them. He thought it was funny of Auntie Becky not to want one.

Chapter 18

Peter was a well-mannered, amiable young man. He distributed his affections pretty equally between Becky and his sports car. And so long as Becky was friendly, as she always was, and so long as his car was running sweetly, which it always did, he found the world a pleasant place to live in.

There was only one thing that occasionally worried him slightly – the knowledge that, if he ever got around to marrying Becky, he would first have to ask the permission of that fire-eating father of hers. For it had always been Peter's policy to give the old man as wide a berth as possible. And the thought of actually having to seek him out and put a proposition to him – it made Peter's blood run cold.

So that when the old gentleman met him on his arrival and ushered him silently into his study, Peter was alarmed. Grandpa shut the door, and said, 'Sit down, young man. I want a word with you.'

Peter perched on the edge of a chair. 'Have a cigar,' said Grandpa, with what he intended for a friendly smile, but which, to Peter's overwrought imagination, came out with all the grinning menace of an African war mask.

Grandpa lit the cigar for him. 'Am I right,' he began in his silkiest tones, 'in thinking that you want to marry my daughter Becky?'

Despite the silkiness, this seemed to Peter a very loaded question. 'Well, er – ' he began.

If there was one thing calculated to take any silkiness out of Grandpa's voice it was shilly-shallying. Shilly-shally with Grandpa and you were lost. 'Well, do you or don't you?' he demanded.

'Ye-es. Yes, sir.'

'Then why the hell don't you?' asked Grandpa.

Peter was so overcome by the unexpectedness of this question that he remained silent. Then he said, 'You – you mean I have your permission, sir?'

'And my blessing dear boy,' said Grandpa, all friendliness once more.

'I say. That's awfully good of you, sir.'

Grandpa rose. He put a hand on Peter's shoulder. 'Go to her, my boy. And may she make you as happy as she has made me.' His voice trembled. He put a hand over his eyes. He had affected himself very deeply.

So Peter sought out Becky, who was draped elegantly over a swing hammock, and cried, 'Becky! The old boy says I can ask you to marry me.'

She set the hammock swinging. 'Can – or must, Peter?'

'Why, can, of course.'

'Tell me what happened,' she said. He told her. 'Well, the cunning old devil,' she said admiringly.

He sat beside her in the swinging hammock. '*Will* you marry me, old girl?' he asked humbly.

'Yes, of course I will,' said the warm-hearted Becky. 'And I don't care if it *was* Father's idea. I still think it was a jolly good one.'

He was hurt. 'It wasn't your father's idea. It was mine.'

'Of course it was, darling. I think six is a nice number, don't you?'

'Six?'

'Children, my pet.'

This was an aspect of marriage that had not occurred to Peter. 'But we should never get them in the car, Becky.'

'Sell the car,' she said. 'And buy a bus.'

Sell the car! Peter felt like a man to whom a flash of lightning has just revealed a dreadful chasm beneath his feet. Then he looked at Becky, and decided that for anyone as beautiful and dear as she, he would sell the car and walk barefoot all his days. Which was really saying quite a lot for Peter.

Momma said to Poppa, 'Guess what. Becky wants Gaylord for a page at her wedding.'

Poppa stared. 'I say, that's taking a bit of a risk, isn't it? And what's he going to wear? I'm not having him dressed up as Little Lord Fauntleroy.'

'I believe they're going to stick him in a kilt. Apparently your maternal great-grandmother organized one or two Highland massacres, so it's quite in order.'

Poppa looked delighted. Like most of the English, he thought the Scots were one of the Almighty's funniest, though perhaps least subtle, jokes. But like every Englishman with a drop of Scottish blood in his veins he was immensely proud of this fact, and he had secret, Walter Mittyish dreams of himself striding along in a kilt, up to the fetlocks in heather. 'A kilt, eh?' he said. 'Yes. Yes. I think that will be very suitable.'

So did Gaylord. He was intrigued. On the morning of the wedding he went to the loo fifteen times, fascinated by this new approach to a humdrum task. Nevertheless, he was ready well before time, not a hair out of place, neck well scrubbed. Momma couldn't believe it. She looked him over, and couldn't find a thing wrong. 'What have you got in your sporran?' she asked, knowing it could well harbour anything from a dead mouse to a quarter of bull's-eyes. But Gaylord fished inside and held up a sixpence. 'Only my collection, Momma,' he said demurely.

Poppa came in, trying to pretend that he felt as much at home in his grey topper and tails as in a sports coat and flannels. Gaylord looked at him in awe and wonder. 'Momma!' he gasped. 'Doesn't Poppa look *super!*'

'Yes,' said Momma, a little short. She was under the impression she didn't look too bad herself. But no one had thought to mention the fact.

Rose came in, still walking in her sleep, in good tweeds and a hat that had all the feminine allure of a motorcycle crash helmet.

'Hello, Rose dear,' said Momma, holding out her hands and smiling.

'Hello, May,' said Rose.

'Cheer up, old girl,' said Poppa, putting his arm about her shoulders.

Grandpa burst in, and was brought up short by the sight of his elder daughter. 'Good God, Rose. This isn't a funeral.'

'Oh, for heaven's sake,' said Poppa.

'Never mind, dear,' Great Aunt Marigold said. 'Mr Right will come along one day.'

Poppa looked at Rose's face. My goodness, she's brave, he thought. To save her further embarrassment he said, 'Come on. Time we were going.'

'Now, Gaylord! Remember!' said Momma, departing.

She could have saved her breath. For Gaylord remembered everything. As he followed his lovely aunt and his really very impressive grandfather down the nave, his bearing was impeccable. And during the service he was more solemn than the priest, more composed than the groom, more correct than the best man. Momma watched her strangely dignified son with a proud, yearning affection that brought tears to her eyes. Today she had discovered a new facet to his character. Gaylord had a sense of Occasion.

After the ceremony she said to Poppa, 'Wasn't he marvellous, darling?'

'Who?'

'Gaylord, of course. I wouldn't have believed a small boy –'

'It's not over yet,' said Poppa. 'Champagne may loosen his tongue.'

But at the reception Gaylord sipped his lemonade with all the aplomb of a diplomat sipping sherry. And made polite conversation when spoken to. And once, alone in a corner, had a dignified little weep when he reflected that, though Uncle Peter was pretty old, it would undoubtedly be several years before he passed on and left his beautiful widow free to marry Gaylord.

Then came the champagne. Gaylord sipped his thimbleful and wrinkled his nose. He wished he'd stuck to lemonade. The cake was a disappointment, too, Gaylord's idea of a helping of cake being a good, solid wedge. This piece the size of a small cigar was no good to anybody. But he did not complain. He ate it with every appearance of dignified enjoyment. To Momma the combination of maternal pride, champagne, and the special euphoria engendered by weddings was quite demoralizing. She fairly drooled over Gaylord. And Gaylord, so co-operative was he determined to be, let her drool.

But now things were moving to a close. Becky had changed out of her white, bridal gown into her going-away things. Peter was back in a lounge suit. The car was waiting.

Everyone trooped out into the summer sunshine to see them off.

It was a happy, light-hearted moment. Everyone was talking nineteen to the dozen, laughing, joking. Even Rose, chatting to a skirted and jumpered friend, looked animated. While Momma, one hand resting on Jocelyn's elegant sleeve, the other holding Gaylord's hot little paw, thought she had never been so proud and happy in her life. And proud, not only of her be-toppered husband and kilted son, but of this whole mad, delightful family into which she had married. Of Grandpa, strong as an ox yet strangely dignified and commanding on this important day. Of Great Aunt Marigold, not quite sure who was marrying who, but being very sweet and gentle and courteous to everyone. Of Becky with her robust, warm beauty, passing on some of her own zest and enjoyment to those less fortunate. Even of Rose, who was so nice if you ever managed to hack your way through the jungle of repressions with which she surrounded herself.

The hubbub was tremendous. Then, gradually, it died. Becky, laughing beside the car, was gesturing for silence. Gradually she got it. Everyone was pleasurably watching those red, laughing lips, those even, white teeth; everyone was waiting for the message.

And it was at this unfortunate moment that Gaylord remembered something. 'Momma,' he asked, loud and clear and serious. 'Why did Auntie Becky say this was a shotgun wedding?'

The silence went on. But it had changed. It was no longer mildly expectant. It was agog.

It was broken by Momma saying calmly, 'She was joking, dear.'

'She wasn't. Momma.' Gaylord was very definite. 'She said to Grandpa, "How dare you threaten me with a shotgun wedding?" And he said, "Call it a shotgun wedding if you like, but you're going to marry that young man before it's too late." He did, Momma.'

'Then I suppose they were both joking,' said Momma.

'They weren't. Momma. It was that day Auntie Rose stabbed her lover.'

Everyone began to laugh and chatter even more gaily, as they pondered this absorbing glimpse of life at the Cypresses. And Momma whispered to Poppa, 'Well, that's given everyone an interest for the next nine months.' But Poppa said, 'Nine months! My dear May, if Becky dies childless at the age of ninety, they'll still think the worst.'

But for Rose it was not funny. It was bad enough that the family should have seen her lose control. But to have that wretched child broadcast it to half the county... Without a word she crept up to her room, and flung her ridiculous hat on the floor, and watched with a bitter heart as the laughing fools gradually drifted away in their sleek motor cars.

Chapter 19

For their summer holidays Momma and Poppa always took Gaylord to the same cottage in Wales between the mountains and the sea. Poppa had a guilt complex about this. Living in an age when the world, or at any rate Europe, could be his annual oyster, it seemed churlish to go on doing what he could have done ever since the 1860s. But he happened to like it.

Often, standing in the dusk of a muddy lane, he would think: Now I could be sipping my wine in the Champs-Elysées, or gazing at the Colosseum. Hearing the sleepy sea, or the drumming of rain on the tin roof, or the music of Welsh voices, he would think, I could be hearing the clack of the castanets, or the surge of great music in Bayreuth, Paris, Vienna. But he knew that then he would not have felt the intense, subtle pleasure of returning to a loved place; of opening the cottage door to be greeted by the smells of geraniums, paraffin, firewood, damp, newspapers, floor polish and a few centuries of simple, earthy, country living. He would not have known the pleasure of going up, tired from the journey, to the great, sprawling bed under the sloping roof, with the promise of a long night's sleep and a long, lazy day tomorrow.

And May liked it. The quiet, the freedom, just the three of them, alone, away from the family. This year, too, it had a greater attraction. At the seaside, far from the Foggerties, Gaylord could be given his freedom once more. Momma and Poppa both believed that one of the best things that could happen to any small boy was to have the lanes and fields and beaches of England for his playground. Though they dared do no other, it had been with great reluctance that they had curbed his wanderings at home. And they both determined that in Wales they would fight down their fears and give him as much freedom as a boy of his age could reasonably expect.

But on another question May had doubts. There was so much that she had – Jocelyn, Gaylord, the privilege and promise of the new life already so vigorous in her body. And Rose, poor Rose had nothing. Nothing at all. May said to Jocelyn, 'I've been thinking. Do you think we ought to ask Rose if she'd like to come with us? She's so utterly wretched, poor girl.'

'Perhaps,' said Poppa hopefully, 'she's got something else arranged.'

'I doubt it. And it won't be much fun for her, just staying here with your father and Aunt Marigold.'

Jocelyn thought. 'I'd rather we went alone,' he said.

'So would I. It does us good to get away from the family. But –'

'I know,' said Jocelyn. '"But –" Have a word with her, darling.'

So May had a word. Rose looked grateful, frightened, even resentful. 'I'm sure you'd rather be on your own,' she said.

'We shouldn't ask you if we didn't want you,' said May. Rose looked as though she were going to cry. 'It's very good of you both.'

'Rubbish. We want you to come.'

'Of course,' said Rose, brightening. 'I could babysit for you in the evenings.'

May felt an unkind desire to hit her sister-in-law over the head. But she said patiently, 'There's only a handful of cottages and a chapel. The night life isn't a feature of the place.'

'Well, I could still take him off your hands in the daytime.'

'Now listen, Rose,' May said firmly. 'If you come, you are coming for a holiday and as our guest. We're not asking you because we want an unpaid nanny or a daily help.'

'It's very kind of you,' Rose said, trying hard to sound relaxed and grateful, but not quite able to keep the brusqueness out of her voice.

'Well?' asked Jocelyn.

'She'll come.'

'Oh, good.' He was genuinely glad – for Rose's sake. He looked at his wife. 'What are you smiling about?'

'Poor old Rose. She had to talk herself into thinking she was doing us a favour before she'd accept.'

And so they came to the cottage. Poppa opened the door – and they might never have been away. The china dogs gazed with smug and rapt expressions from the inglenook. The geraniums still stood in the two-foot-deep window embrasure. And there were the photographs, in their velvet frames, of Blackpool Tower, and the late Mr Davies, and a prize bull. It was all there, it had all been there, waiting through the long and changing year. Poppa carried the cases upstairs, Gaylord went off to the beach. Rose said, 'Now, May, you relax and I'll get a meal ready. It won't take two minutes.'

With a sinking heart May realized that Rose was putting on her Girl Guide Act. For the next fortnight Rose was going to be determinedly cheerful, eager, and just too bloody helpful for words. Given half a chance she would organize them all – and Momma knew well how Jocelyn hated being organized. The only way to organize Jocelyn was the way she did it, so that he never knew.

Gaylord returned, caked with sand, his hair and skin crisped already with salt and sun. 'Well,' Poppa said. 'Is it still there?'

'What?'

'The sea,' said Poppa.

Gaylord realized Poppa had made a joke. He grinned appreciatively. He liked Poppa to make jokes, not because of their amusement-rating, which was usually pretty low, but because it showed they were not failing to see eye to eye. Then Auntie Rose said, 'Come on, everybody. Tea. Then afterwards I'll see to the washing-up while you all go and have a look at the briny.'

'What's the briny?' asked Gaylord.

'The sea, dear.'

'Never heard it called that before,' said Gaylord.

No, you haven't, thank God, thought Poppa. And Momma thought, why is it that, when some women get all gay and over-excited, the slang of the last generation but one comes bubbling up out of their unconscious.

But Gaylord was off on another tack. 'You remember that gentleman who came at Christmas with Auntie Rose's lover?' he said.

'Stan Grebbie, you mean?' cried Rose. And then, to hide her eagerness. 'I – I think that was his name.'

'He's on the beach,' said Gaylord.

'Oh, Gaylord, don't be so ridiculous,' said Momma. But the effect on Auntie Rose was remarkable. The dreadful phony Girl Guide Act fell from her. She flushed a dull purple. 'Gaylord, are you sure?' she asked, almost pleadingly.

'Course,' said Gaylord.

Momma and Poppa had seen the change in Rose. So that's the way the wind blows, they both thought. Momma said gently, 'Gaylord's not terribly reliable. Rose. He saw Prince Philip coming out of the Shepherd's Warning tobacconist's the other week.'

'It *was* him,' said the disgruntled Gaylord.

'He,' corrected Poppa. 'Who, dear?' asked Momma. 'Prince Philip or Mr Grebbie?'

'Both,' said Gaylord. You could have ledged a penny on his lower lip.

Rose was reducing her paper napkin to shreds. 'It's – it's too much of a coincidence,' she muttered, hoping and praying someone would contradict her. Her prayer was answered. 'These things do happen,' Poppa said. 'I suggest Rose goes and does a recce after tea. If he is staying here we're not likely to miss him.'

'Well, perhaps I will,' said Rose, 'if no one's any objection.' A little of her arch gaiety returned. 'It really would be a coincidence, wouldn't it.'

As soon as tea was finished Rose said, 'Look, May, I'll just wash up. Then perhaps I *will* have a little stroll.'

'You'll go now,' said Momma, no nonsense.

So Rose stepped out into the evening lanes, and hurried to the vast, lonely stretch of sand. Let it be him, she prayed, remembering his shy smile and the pressure of his hand. Let it be him.

The sun was near its setting. The sea stirred no more than a sleeping cat. The tiny crabs scuttled in the rock pools, and the jellyfish glistened in the thin crochet-work of the sea's edge. But of man there was no sign. This might have been the world before that tempestuous creature arrived on it; or after he had taken his departure. Sand, rocks, sea; and the armoured crab, who had seen man come and would see him go, the armoured crab reaching out both ways almost to eternity.

A chill breeze came and ruffled the rock pools, and flung a gritty handful of sand against Rose's legs. She shivered. No one could call Rose over-imaginative; but standing there, on this silent and deserted shore, she had a panic feeling that she was alone; that behind her, and in the lands beyond that quiet sea, there was suddenly no one. Never again would she know the music of human voices in a lighted room. Never again would she know the comfort of another's presence.

She wanted to scream. She must get back to the cottage, reassure herself. She turned and began to run wildly. But the soft sand pulled at her feet, she could make no headway. And the sun was sinking. Once let the light go and she was lost. Here, on this darkling shore, the sea would rear up and drag her down to its cold heart. Things – horrible, unspeakable things – would heave themselves up out of the waves…

This is madness, she thought. The strain of the past months, the awful hopelessness, and emptiness, the knowledge that she had once behaved like a madwoman, never knowing when she was going to run into the hated Bobs, the final disappointment of this evening – it had all been too much for her. She made herself stand still. She had been floundering and nailing along, head down, moaning quietly to herself. Now she stood, and slowly raised her head, forcing herself to take command.

There was a man standing at the top of the slipway. He began to walk slowly down. Then he broke into a run. She too ran, lightly now. They came together. He was beaming foolishly. 'Rose,' he cried. 'So it really is you.'

'Mr Grebbie,' she panted.

They should have come together joyfully, with a kiss. That was what they both wanted. But they were too shy. Nevertheless, they stood very close, holding hands, breathing heavily from their running. 'I thought I saw your little nephew,' he said. 'But I didn't think it could be.'

She gasped, 'He – said he'd seen you. But I – couldn't believe it. It seemed – too much of a coincidence.'

'They say truth's stranger than fiction,' he said. It was not a brilliantly original remark. But Rose thought it was very apt. They went on smiling at each other. He was less grey than she remembered him. He was wearing a blue shirt and flannels, and the wind and sea had slapped some colour into his cheeks. 'How long are you staying?' she asked.

He looked at her ruefully. 'Only till tomorrow evening,' he said.

Rose's eyes filled with tears. She just couldn't help it. She was no great believer in either God or Fate. But since one or the other had gone to all the trouble of bringing her and Mr Grebbie together in this remote spot, she did think whichever it was might have seen that it was for more than twenty-four hours. If they'd been organizing it for Becky, she thought bitterly, they'd have taken care to make it a month.

Stan Grebbie boldly took her arm, and they began to walk. 'I'm afraid it's not very long,' he said. 'We'd better make the most of it.'

'Yes,' she said. They strolled towards the sea. Now that the sun had gone down the world had suddenly flared into life. Sea and sky burned like a bonfire. She gazed hungrily. Then she turned and saw the sunset mirrored in his eyes. Well, there was still this evening. And tomorrow. Twenty-four hours deducted unexpectedly from a lifetime of spinsterhood. It was the most she could hope for. It was more than she *had* hoped for. 'Where are you staying?' she asked, suddenly content, feeling herself drained of emotion as the sky was now once more draining itself of colour.

'With a couple called Williams, near the Chapel. But a friend of mine's calling for me tomorrow, in his car, and we're going to tour Ireland.'

Do you have to go, she wondered. But she knew instinctively that for Stan Grebbie an arrangement would be an arrangement. If he had told a friend he was going to Ireland with him, then not all the seduction of the sirens could have stopped him, let alone poor Rose, who had no lures.

'From Holyhead?' she asked, not caring.

'Yes. We're catching the night boat. Taking the car across with us.' But he didn't sound as though he cared, either. 'I wish I wasn't going now. Rose.'

'Do you really?'

'Yes,' he said, and put his arm about her waist.

And Rose knew no fear, no inhibitions. Whatever Stan did, or wanted to do, would be right. She put from her mind all doubts, conflicts, decisions. She put up her face, with a smile of infinite love and trust. He looked at her in wonder, then, very gravely, he kissed her, under the washed and empty sky.

'I told you it was him, didn't I, Auntie Rose,' said a self-satisfied young voice. They sprang apart. 'I knew it was, the moment I saw him on the beach.'

'Why, hello, young man,' cried Mr Grebbie trying to sound pleased. But Rose made no attempt to hide her disappointment. Every minute of this twenty-four hours was a jewel – a jewel she would carry all her life. She dare not waste one. 'It's time you were in bed, Gaylord,' she said.

'Momma said I could stay up.' Gaylord quoted the supreme authority with satisfaction. He turned to Mr Grebbie. 'Would you like me to show you a cave, Mr Grebbie?'

'Not tonight, young man,' said Stan.

Gaylord skipped along beside them. 'What shall we do tomorrow?'

They were silent. Each had been making plans. But in the unspoken plans of neither was Gaylord included. Rose said, 'Mr Grebbie and I have not yet decided whether we are doing anything tomorrow.'

'Perhaps Mr Grebbie and I could go for a picnic,' said Gaylord. 'Momma would pack you some sandwiches,' he assured his new-found friend.

Rose and Stan began to realize, with sinking hearts, that Gaylord had formed an affection for Mr Grebbie. And Gaylord was not one easily to desert the object of his affection. 'Sure you don't want to see that cave?' he asked kindly.

'Sure, thank you,' said Stan.

Rose felt desperately in her handbag. 'Here. Go and buy yourself some sweets at the Post Office.'

'They'll be shut,' said Gaylord.

'Well, go and try,' said Rose.

He turned into a jet aircraft, and went. They watched him. 'He'll be back in ten minutes, at that rate,' she said.

'If he comes back.'

'You don't know Gaylord,' she said. 'Leeches have nothing on that boy.' And then, to her own surprise, she laughed – a gay, girlish laugh. 'Oh, Stan. It is lovely seeing you again.'

But he wasn't listening. 'We could,' he add, 'take evasive action.'

'Where?'

'Those dunes,' he said. 'Come on.'

Gaylord came into the lamplit cottage. 'Auntie Rose sent me to buy some sweets at the Post Office. But they were shut.'

'So – ?' asked Momma, realizing her son wasn't simply imparting useless information.

'So I thought you might have some.'

'Here you are,' she said, giving him a bag.

'Thanks, Momma.' He made for the door. 'Where are you going?' Poppa asked.

'I'm going to give one to Auntie Rose and Mr Grebbie.'

'Oh no, you're not,' said Momma. 'If it really was Mr Grebbie, they won't want you.'

And that, thought Gaylord, was just where Momma was wrong. Auntie Rose and Mr Grebbie seemed a bit lost on their own. Aimless. They needed him to show them a few places of local interest – caves and things. 'They're *expecting* me,' he said indignantly.

'Gaylord,' said Momma. 'Sit down.'

He perched mutinously on the edge of a chair. Momma said, 'While you are on holiday your father and I want you to have as much freedom as possible, because when we get home you'll still have to go about with us.'

For a few brief hours Gaylord had almost forgotten Willie's brothers. Now he remembered them, and the old, familiar fears stirred in him.

'But we are not having you wandering about in the dusk,' went on Momma. 'And you mustn't inflict yourself on Auntie Rose and Mr Grebbie. They'll have a lot to talk about.'

'They haven't,' said Gaylord. 'They were hardly saying a word.'

But had he seen them at that moment he would have been surprised to find that they did not seem to be missing him at all. Laughing, hand in hand, they ran across the wet, rippled sand of the sea's edge, and crouched conspiratorially in the dunes like a couple of children; a man and a woman, nearing middle-age, pathetic, slightly ridiculous; both lonely, both frightened to death by ordinary, confident people; each suddenly finding in the other the solace and comfort they had never thought to find. Even the running to hide from a small boy had been symbolic. So would they wish to hide together, in a place of refuge, from the harsh world of men. So would they each be comforted and protected by the weakness of the other.

They stayed a long time in the sheltering dunes, while a great Chinese lantern of a moon sailed up over the land of Wales. And when at last they came home, to the pale lights of the cottages, they both knew that they had found a refuge from the world.

Rose walked home with her head among the stars. She came into the cottage, and stood blinking in the lamp light. Jocelyn was alone in the inglenook, smoking a last pipe. He gave her his slow smile. 'Well, I gather it was indeed Mr Grebbie.'

'Yes,' she said. 'Isn't it extraordinary!'

He looked at her, still smiling. What was even more extraordinary, he thought, was the effect on Rose. She looked as though she had cast a skin. For the first time he saw a resemblance to Becky. And all because a grey, no longer young school teacher had turned up on a lonely beach. Jocelyn was a kind man, but an honest one. 'He's a nice chap,

Grebbie,' he said. He couldn't, in honesty, say much more. He couldn't, in kindness, say much less.

But Rose's face had lit up. 'Oh, I am glad you like him, Jocelyn. He's – he really is a very fine person. Don't you think so?'

'To be frank, I prefer him to that other chap,' Jocelyn said. 'How long is he staying?'

Rose's face fell. 'He's leaving tomorrow, at teatime.'

Blast, thought Jocelyn. Poor old Rose. It really was time she had a break. 'I'm sorry,' he said.

'So am I.' She gave him a rueful smile.

He sighed. 'You must make the most of tomorrow.'

'We're going to,' she said simply.

Chapter 20

It was one of those gay, fresh mornings that happen only at the seaside. The breeze was just a little out of hand. The willows trembled, and the undersides of their leaves were like a shower of bright pennies. The sky was littered with clouds at all levels. Fat little clouds that bounced about the foothills, streamers, trailing from the peaks, and a few ostrich feathers in the high reaches of the sky.

Rose and her love strode briskly through the flat, reedy, watery land. They had until five o'clock this afternoon. And, in this moment of time, everything took on a fearful clarity. In the clear, cool morning light they saw things as a man about to die sees them; as though seeing them, not for the last, but for the first time. They saw the joyous surge of the cold green sea, they saw the clean, simple beauty of a white gull against a blue sky. They saw the long, empty day stretching like a white road before them, and were glad. They saw the sun travelling remorselessly to its quenching in the western sea; and they were filled with fears.

Mr Grebbie had an old gas mask case filled with sandwiches and a thermos. They were bound for another beach; one where, they fondly hoped, even Gaylord would not find them.

Rose thought: surely he'll say something, today. Surely he won't just go off to Ireland and then back to a new term in

County Durham, and nothing said. I love him, I think he loves me. We can't let it end like this, just because we're both too shy to say, 'I love you, I want you for the rest of my life.'

'Stan,' she said.

'Yes?'

'I wish we didn't live so far apart,' she said tremulously.

'So do I,' he said. 'I – I shall miss you. Rose.'

'Will you, really?'

'Yes, rather.' But now they were in sight of the little bay. And they both saw something that chilled their blood. A small boy, fishing in a rock pool. 'Why on earth should he choose this bay?' said Rose.

'There's another little beach just along the road,' he said.

They plodded on. It was no distance. But this was a more popular beach, noisy with children, gay with brightly coloured towels and chairs and swimsuits. There was even an ice-cream van and a man with boats. 'Oh, dear,' said Mr Grebbie. 'It looks a bit crowded.'

He spread his mackintosh. They sat down, but found they were at silly mid-on to a vigorous cricket match. They moved. A dog came and sniffed at them with critical detachment. A fat child, spade in one hand bucket in the other, stood and stared at them owlishly. Rose flapped at him as at a wasp. 'Go away,' she said disgustedly.

The child did not react, just went on staring. He looked as though he could keep it up for days. 'We might as well be at Blackpool,' Rose said, with a sound that was half laugh, half sob.

He put his hand over hers. He looked anxiously about him. But there seemed no escape. To the right of this tiny, crowded bay was the devoted Gaylord. To the left, a tumble of boulders that reached to a far headland. Behind, the boggy, reedy waste. It was already midday. There must be somewhere they could find peace and loneliness, without walking back to last night's empty beach.

Then he had an idea. 'I know. Let's take a boat out.'

'Oh, Stan. That would be lovely.' Rose, who had been looking unbelievably miserable, brightened.

But now he was being afflicted by doubts. 'I'm afraid I'm not a practised oarsman,' he said. 'But the sea looks reasonably calm.'

'It's like a mill pond,' she said. 'Come on.'

They hurried down to the boats. The man in charge began to drag one down to the sea. And then Rose said, out of the corner of her mouth, 'Don't look now, but Gaylord's just coming round the point.'

'Oh, God,' said Stan. Feverishly he and Rose began to push the boat seaward, to the intense annoyance of the boatman, who was not given to rush and bustle. 'What is it, then? Not launching the lifeboat, are we?' he asked reprovingly.

They ignored him, and floundered aboard. The oars wielded by Stan, whirled like demented semaphores. But at last he got them settled in the rowlocks. He was braced for a long, strong pull.

And it was then that they heard the first, heart-rending yell. 'Auntie Rose. Wait for me. Auntie Rose.'

Rose stiffened, but did not turn round. Grebbie stared with awful concentration at the tip of his right oar.

'Auntie Rose. Wait!' The cry was anguished.

It was no good. She turned round. Like a shark at the smell of blood Gaylord was coming through the shallows. Defeatedly they pulled him aboard. He sat, puffing and grinning delightedly. 'Wasn't it a bit of luck,' he said, 'me just seeing you like that.'

'Luck for whom?' asked Rose nastily.

'Everybody,' said Gaylord. Lucky for him because he loved boats. Lucky for Auntie Rose and Mr Grebbie because it would have been a bit dull for them just rowing about on their own. He looked at Stan in admiration. 'I didn't know Mr Grebbie could row,' he said.

Neither did Mr Grebbie. And yet, although his strokes felt to him quite ineffectual, it was surprising how far they had already travelled. The little bay was now a small part of a long coastline, backed by purple mountains. Rose looked behind her. 'I think it's time we stopped and ate our sandwiches.'

'Yes,' said Stan, relieved.

Rose looked at her watch. Two o'clock. Only as long as from eleven o'clock, and this lovely day would be over. Everything would be over. She just couldn't bear it. 'Stan,' she said.

He heard the break in her voice. He looked at her. She was gazing at him with a pleading tenderness that moved him deeply.

Gaylord was leaning over the stern, trailing his hands in the exquisitely cold water. All that could be seen of him was his sturdy legs and the seat of his khaki shorts. It was now or never. 'Rose,' Stan whispered urgently. 'Rose. I love you. Will you – ?'

He had leaned forward to take her hand. His right oar, abandoned, slid gently into the water and floated away at a surprising speed.

Gaylord heard the splash. He turned, and took in the whole entrancing situation in one joyous glance. 'How did it happen, Mr Grebbie?' he asked. 'You must have let go, did you?'

Auntie Rose said, 'Be quiet, Gaylord. Let Mr Grebbie think.'

Mr Grebbie thought. 'We *must* get it back,' he moaned. He had seen men propel boats by waggling an oar in the water at the stern. He tried. The attempt was singularly unsuccessful. 'It's getting *ever* such a long way away,' said Gaylord.

He was right, of course. That damned oar was bobbing off down St George's Channel like a sheep that has wandered through a gap in the hedge. And in some strange way the coastline too seemed to be slipping further and further away. Mr Grebbie had always imagined that seafaring men's absorption with tides was something of an affectation. Now suddenly, he wished he knew a bit more about them.

Rose, on the other hand, was thinking: his friend's calling for him at five. If we don't get rescued pretty soon the whole arrangement's going to fall through. So she would wait a bit before leading any hymns for those in peril on the sea. 'I think we should just sit here quietly and eat our sandwiches,' she said.

Gaylord, in whose world of the imagination all this was a routine occurrence, said, 'We may be adrift for days and days. I think we ought to save our provisions.'

'Now look,' said Rose. 'We're about half a mile off the Welsh coast; not in the middle of the Pacific. And I'm hungry. I'm having a sandwich.'

They ate their sandwiches. Gaylord finished off his own, and then helped Rose and Stan to eat theirs, while at the same time giving them an uneasy feeling of improvidence. When they had finished every crumb, and finished off the coffee, he said chattily, 'People in open boats sometimes eat each other.' He thought it was a good thing he'd come along. He didn't really think Auntie Rose and Mr Grebbie, on their

170

own, would have had much of a clue in a situation like this.

Grebbie said, 'Oh, Rose. I do feel an awful fool.'

'Don't be silly,' she said. 'It could have happened anyone.'

Gaylord said, 'I bet it wouldn't have happened to Poppa. He's *ever* such a good rower.'

'It could happen to anyone,' Rose said firmly. But Gaylord was staring at the sea. 'There's the oar,' he said.

They looked. Current or wind had brought the oar floating back almost beside them. Rose felt a sudden disappointment. Given that oar, they could still be home by five. Without it they might drift, in no very great danger, for hours. And she liked drifting. Without Gaylord, just the two of them, it would have been very heaven. Even with Gaylord it was pleasant. But the officious child was already half overboard, struggling to reach the oar. Rose instinctively grabbed his legs. 'Hold tight. Auntie Rose,' he said. 'I think I can reach it.'

She watched his splayed fingers almost touching the oar. Then the bouncing waves brought it yet closer. Gaylord's fingers touched the wood – and at that moment Auntie Rose loosened her grip and he almost went overboard. Almost, but not quite. His fingers, however, instead of grasping the oar, knocked it away. It went bobbing off once more.

'Oh, bad luck, old chap,' said Mr Grebbie.

But Gaylord was furious. 'Auntie Rose let me go,' he said. 'Just when I'd nearly got it.' Really, women!

'I was trying to let you reach out a bit further,' said Rose.

Grebbie said piteously, 'What you must think of me, Rose! I'm the very last man to cope with a situation like this.

Come to that, I'm the very last man to be trusted with a boat.'

'There's nothing anyone could do,' she said gently. 'We're sure to be picked up before nightfall.'

'I don't see why,' said Gaylord. 'We're miles and miles from land, now.'

They waited. 'That oar's right out of sight now,' said Gaylord.

They waited. They shouted in chorus. They tied Gaylord's shirt to the oar and waved it. Nothing happened. 'I think I can see Ireland,' said Gaylord.

Time passed. It was four o'clock. Earth and sea and clouds and sky took on the slightly shop-soiled look of late afternoon. Already there was a touch of chill in the sea breeze. 'I shouldn't think we shall be rescued now,' Gaylord observed cheerfully.

Rose couldn't have cared less. She was resting in the crook of Stan's arm, occasionally smiling up into his serious, anxious face. 'Cheer up, Stan,' she laughed. 'We're not going to die, you know.'

Gaylord wondered where she got that idea from. 'Is that a vulture?' he asked hopefully, pointing to a seagull.

They were rescued at five-fifteen, by the reproachful boatman in a motor-boat. Gaylord was faintly disgusted. Not even a helicopter. And the chances now of Auntie Rose and Mr Grebbie and himself drawing lots to see who should eat whom seemed sadly remote. He was beginning to learn that the world of reality seldom measures up to the world of the imagination.

Nevertheless, he had a tale to tell. As soon as they landed he said politely, 'Excuse me, Mr Grebbie, goodbye,' and he turned into a Mark 10 Jaguar and streaked home down the fast lane of the M1.

They ought to have been home half an hour ago. And they had a mile in front of them. 'Will your friend wait?' Rose asked.

Grebbie looked worried to death. 'I don't really think he will. He's got one of those very quick tempers.'

'Oh, good,' Rose said absently.

He looked at her in surprise. 'Anyway, our passages were booked. And if he wasn't away from here soon after five he'd miss the boat.'

It was a gentle evening. Rose felt a strange content, a sense of oneness with the hills, and the coarse turf beneath her feet and the shy, kindly man at her side. She said, 'You were just saying something when that oar slipped away, Stan.'

He was silent. Then he said bitterly, 'You wouldn't want a nincompoop like me to – say that again.'

She pressed her head back against his shoulder. 'I would Stan.'

He disengaged himself almost roughly. He sounded as angry with her as with himself. 'I couldn't ask anyone to marry me. I can't even look after myself, let alone a wife.' He strode along scowling, his head down, hands in pockets.

She hurried wretchedly by his side. 'But if I'm willing to take the risk, surely – ' She laughed nervously.

He shook his head, and said nothing. He glanced at his watch. 'I even let my friends down.'

She knew she could do nothing with him while he was in this mood of bitter self-contempt. She must simply be patient, hope that his friend had gone without him, and then try to win him round during the ensuing fortnight.

At last they came to the cottage, and a Mrs Williams fairly effervescing with bad news. 'Oh, very put out, he was, Mr Grebbie. Went off in a huff, and no mistake.'

Stan stood pulling at his lower lip. Then he straightened his dejected shoulders. 'Well, I certainly don't blame him,' he said.

Mrs Williams went back into the cottage, very satisfied with the way her news had been received. Stan said, 'I'm sorry, Rose. I'm – afraid I've not been very good company.'

'Stan,' she said. 'I've got something to tell you. It was my fault Gaylord didn't reach that oar. I let him slip.'

He wasn't very interested. 'That's nice of you to say so, Rose. But if I hadn't lost it in the first place – '

She said earnestly, 'But I did it on purpose. Because I wanted to keep you here. That's what I'm telling you.'

He gave her a look that frightened her. 'Well, that was a friendly thing to do, I must say.'

'Why, you said yourself you – wished you weren't going to Ireland.'

'I may have done. But if there's one thing I cannot stand it's breaking an arrangement.' He stood there, staring at the distant mountains, his grey hair blowing in the evening breeze. She too gazed at the faraway hills. 'Shall you be staying on here?'

'I suppose so. There's not much else, is there?'

'Then I'll probably see you,' she said. 'Good night, Stan.'

'Good night,' he said, turning into the cottage.

She walked home with a heavy heart. What a situation! If a man didn't love you, you could at least try to influence him in your favour. But if he loved you, yet thought so ill of himself that he wouldn't propose marriage, what did you do then? Propose it yourself? Well, she'd virtually done that, And got nowhere. So the only consolation was that they were both going to spend the next fortnight in the same tiny village. She had a fortnight in which to coax, bully, or lure Stan Grebbie into marriage.

'We were going to draw lots,' said Gaylord, coming to the end of a long saga. The Ancient Mariner had nothing on him.

'Whatever for?' asked Momma.

'To see who ate who, of course.'

'Whom,' corrected Poppa.

Momma looked at Poppa. 'Do we believe a word of this?'

Gaylord said, 'Well, you can ask Auntie Rose.' He was affronted. Something really exciting happened – and they just refused to believe you. 'I could see Ireland from where we were,' he said.

'I'm surprised you couldn't see the Manhattan skyline,' said Momma.

'I did,' said Gaylord, who didn't know what it was but was game for anything. 'In the distance,' he admitted.

'Well, we shall just have to wait and see what Auntie Rose has to say,' said Momma.

'It sounds like her now,' said Poppa.

But it wasn't Rose. It was a telegraph boy. And the telegram said, 'Marigold died this morning. Father.'

Jocelyn was in the living-room, alone. 'Where's May?' Rose asked.

Jocelyn said, 'She's upstairs, packing. Aunt Marigold's dead.'

Rose sat down rather heavily. 'When are we going?'

'Tomorrow morning,' said Jocelyn. 'I wanted to go alone at first, but May insists on coming. And Gaylord seems to think a death in the family is something not to be missed on any account.' He gave her his slow smile.

Rose said in a high, tight voice, 'Do we have to go, Jocelyn?'

He looked at her in surprise. 'I think we should. The old man had a great affection for her, you know. He's going to feel it. Besides, her death diminishes him.'

'Yes,' she said, twisting her handkerchief into a tight little ball. 'Yes. Father's going to miss her a lot.'

'I'm sorry, Rose,' he said, wondering at her distress. 'But I think we ought to go.'

'Yes, of course.'

'After all, Mr Grebbie's gone too, hasn't he.'

'No,' she said. 'He's staying after all. That's – that's why – it's all a bit of a shock.' Her face was working painfully. 'I know I shouldn't think about that. I ought to be thinking about Aunt Marigold and poor Father. But – I always was a selfish bitch.'

Jocelyn put his arm round her. Poor old Rose, he thought. The first time anything worked out right for her would be the first time. 'You're going to stay,' he said. 'I'll explain to Father. You can have the cottage, and everyone will be able to say how improper and unfilial it all is.'

'Thanks, Jocelyn,' she said. 'But I couldn't.'

'You can and will,' he said.

She shook her head. 'I don't think I want to, Jocelyn. I'm – not in the mood any more.'

He looked at her in surprise. 'Things not turning out too well?'

'Afraid not. Perhaps we're both too old to be prepared to take the risk. I – don't know.'

'I still think you ought to stay,' he said quietly.

She shook her head. 'No. I'm coming, Jocelyn. If he wants to find me, he knows where I live. But – somehow – I don't think he will.'

After supper she went to tell Stan they were leaving. But Mrs Williams said he had gone to bed early, and she obviously wasn't going to risk any impropriety by doing anything whatever about it. So Rose left a note; but when they came away in the morning, Mr Grebbie was not there to see them off.

Chapter 21

They broke their journey in Chester. Gaylord, who had ten shillings holiday money still unspent, gazed in the shop windows with longing. The desire to spend ten shillings was overwhelming. But they were not very interesting shops; all ladies' clothes and old sort of furniture.

And then, in one of the old-sort-of-furniture shops, he saw it – and could not believe his eyes. Momma and Poppa and Auntie Rose, returning to the car, were naturally irritated that Gaylord should hold them up by staring goggle-eyed at the window of an antique shop. 'Come *along*, Gaylord,' cried Momma.

But Gaylord, for once, was beyond speech. He simply went on staring.

'He's just doing it to annoy,' said Poppa. 'There can't be anything in a shop like that to interest him.'

But in the end the mountains had to go back to Mohammed. Poppa said, 'Gaylord, we've still got a hundred miles – '

'Look,' said Gaylord, stubbing a finger against the plate glass.

They looked. 'Good Lord,' said Poppa. 'A glass paper-weight.'

'I didn't know you could *buy* them, in shops,' said Gaylord. It was like seeing a rainbow up for sale.

But Momma's brain was doing a combination-lock act. Tumblers were falling into place. 'Is that what you wanted for Christmas?' she asked.

But Gaylord was already marching into the shop. 'How – how much is that paperweight?' he asked, breathless with excitement.

'Ten shillings,' said the assistant. And he made Gaylord's day by adding, 'Sir.' It was that sort of shop.

Gaylord groped in the pockets of his shorts, and placed on the elegant counter a collection of sea shells, sixpences, bits of string, toffee papers, threepenny pieces, pebbles and coppers. Together he and the shop assistant sorted out ten shillings. Gaylord shovelled the rest back. The man put the paperweight in a box, wrapped it, and held the door open. Gaylord sailed out like royalty. 'He called me "Sir",' he told his astonished parents.

Back in the car he opened the box and gazed entranced. Instead of Leeds Town Hall this one had a picture of a river with swans and willows, but otherwise it was the same; smooth, rounded, lucent. Gaylord gazed at it from all angles, and decided it was beautiful whichever way you looked at it. And then a mean, sly, crafty voice somewhere in his head whispered, 'Willie would like that.'

Gaylord pretended he hadn't heard. But he began to feel a bit depressed. Then Momma said, 'Let me see, Gaylord.'

He handed it to Momma. She held it delicately in her long fingers. 'It *is* pretty, isn't it,' she said.

'Yes,' said Gaylord. And again that nasty, furtive voice whispered, 'Willie would like that.'

'Well, he's not having it,' said Gaylord, sticking his lower lip out.

'But Willie hasn't any other toys,' persisted the voice. 'You've got lots. And poor Willie is only ninepence to the shilling.'

'He's not having it,' Gaylord said again, more aggressively but with less conviction.

The voice was silent. They were nearly home before it suddenly said, 'Think what a nice, generous boy Willie would find you if you gave it him.'

Now an adult has had years of experience of dealing with the promptings of a starry-eyed conscience. He can trot out a hundred arguments against the proposed course of action. But Gaylord had had no such experience. He stuck his hands in his pockets, sprawled miserably over the back seat, and promised to think about it.

But the thought of Willie had intensified thoughts that even the brisk sea air had not been able to drive from his mind. Willie's brothers would still be waiting for him when he got home again. He felt frightened. He wished he'd stayed at the seaside, after all. You were safe there. But one day, however careful he was, one day he would turn a corner and they would be there, silent, unmoving, hands in pockets, staring at him. And when that moment came it would be the beginning of hurt and fear.

They came out of the hot sunshine into the darkened hall. Out of life into the shadow of death. Grandpa met them. 'Hello, May. Hello, Jocelyn. Sorry to bring you back.' His voice had a friendly, melancholy warmth.

'That's all right, Father.' Jocelyn put a hand on the old man's shoulder. 'We're only sorry it happened.' He looked at his father. Yes, in some way difficult to define he had shrunk a little. Some essence had gone out of him. Never send to know for whom the bell tolls...

Gaylord, crossing the landing, found that a certain closed door had a quite irresistible fascination for him. Slowly, very slowly, he edged towards it. He put his hand on the knob.

Rather to his surprise the knob turned and the door opened just like any ordinary, everyday door. Very slowly, on tiptoe, holding his breath, he advanced towards the bed.

Great Aunt Marigold lay there in awful majesty. Gaylord regarded her with considerable interest. She was at once less and more than Aunt Marigold had ever been. Brittle, waxen, stern, imperious. He had an ecstatic fear that she might suddenly sit up and gibber. Nevertheless, he put out a finger and gently prodded the old, cold cheek. It was his hail and farewell. He began to back towards the door, keeping his eyes fixed on Aunt Marigold. Not for all the riches of Aladdin's cave would he have turned his back on that incalculable object.

A voice behind him whispered, 'Gaylord, you shouldn't have come here. Not on your own.' Momma's hands came down protectively over his shoulders. Mother and son stood there, while May gazed with sorrow and compassion at one who had been so well prepared by life for the loneliness of death. Then she looked down at Gaylord. He met her gaze with an expression she could not define – awe, wonder, fear? Then together, silently, hand in hand they came out of the room.

Chapter 22

'You'd get a great deal of pleasure out of giving it to Willie,' said the voice. 'He'd be so grateful you'd feel a bit like God.'

That was all very well. But the menace of the young Foggerties lay like a blight on the whole sweet countryside. Gaylord didn't want to go out alone. He was beginning to hate these peaceful lanes, to dread the watchful quiet of the fields.

On the other hand, the house was full of people and no one was taking much notice of him. He had every opportunity to slip out unobserved. And his conscience had seen to it that the only possible way he could get pleasure from his paperweight now was by giving it to his friend.

So he went, and found Willie in the old quarry as usual. 'You been to the seaside?' Willie asked.

'Yes,' said Gaylord. 'I've brought you a present back.' He gave Willie the box, and waited, watching the pale moon-face eagerly.

It looked as though the excitement of getting a present might be almost too much for Willie. He flushed deeply. His breathing was painful. His fingers trembled as he tore and scratched at the paper. Then he got it open – and stared in devastating disappointment. 'What's it for?' he asked.

Gaylord's heart sank. 'It's a paperweight,' he said. 'Like the one you lost.'

Willie's eyes narrowed. 'The one you pinched, you mean.'

'I didn't, Willie. But I've brought you another one to – to make up for it.'

Willie looked at it almost with disgust. 'This one's no good. You can see the river any day. That other one had a town, streets and things.'

This was what came of listening to conscience. Gaylord didn't feel in the least like God. And it didn't seem to have done Willie much good either. Gaylord said, 'Right. I'll have it back if you don't like it.'

Willie looked crafty. His hand came up over the bauble. Gaylord was about to snatch; and then he saw something that turned his knees to water. Willie's brothers were filing without a word into the quarry. They looked as though they meant business.

The family was gathering. The house was full. In death, Great Aunt Marigold had acquired an importance she never attained to in her unassuming life. Bea and Ben were there, strangely subdued. Becky, lovelier than ever, Peter. Relations who had themselves been waiting for years to take the same journey as Marigold.

There was a knock on the door. Rose answered it. It was Stan.

He did not smile, but looked at her anxiously. 'Come in,' she said. 'I thought you were in Wales.'

'There didn't seem much point in staying. So I'm on my way home.'

'How nice of you to call,' she said, not formally, but as though she thought it was wonderful of him. He still stood on the doorstep; a white crash helmet perched on his head. He held a pair of gauntlets in one hand and slapped them nervously against the other. 'I wanted to say how sorry I was about your aunt.'

'Do come in,' she said, terrified that at any moment he might leap on his scooter and scorch away to County Durham.

He shook his head. 'You've got a house full of people,' he said. 'Sure to have.'

It was true. There wouldn't be much chance of a quiet chat indoors today – even assuming that he wanted one. Then she had an idea. 'Look,' she said. 'I was just going into the village. Why not stroll in with me?'

He looked doubtful. 'I mustn't be long. I don't know the road from here.'

'Come on,' she said, giving him a smile that hid the dreadful anxiety in her heart.

The silence in the old quarry was oppressive. Willie's brothers moved slowly in on Gaylord.

He stood there, with the sun burning down on him, and watched them come. His eyes watched every menacing movement. Their eyes never left his face.

He stood there, small, defiant, helpless; feet planted square, shoulders held desperately straight, chin out.

They were all about him, now, very close. The dry, dusty smell of old clothes, the sharp smell of sweat and bodies, seemed to fill the quarry. Escape was impossible. If he had moved an inch any way he would have come up against one of them.

Bert's face was an inch from Gaylord's. His lip curled in what was with him a characteristic prelude to speech. 'Your dad's a bastard,' he said.

Gaylord stood like a statue. The sweat was pouring into his eyes, but he dare not blink it away lest they think he was crying.

Bert said, 'Say "My dad's a bloody bastard." Go on, say it.'

Gaylord was silent.

Slowly Bert lifted his foot. Then, viciously and deliberately he kicked Gaylord on the shin. 'Say, "My dad's a bloody bastard," ' he repeated.

Everything was going black. The quarry was beginning, very slowly, to gyrate. The pain was surging up into his entire body. He remained silent.

Bert's control broke. 'Say it,' he screamed. 'Go on, say it. Say "My dad's – " ' He hit Gaylord between the eyes.

Gaylord crumpled up, and Bert kicked him, savagely, viciously, until even his brothers were scared and dragged him away. And Gaylord lay sticky with blood in the hot sun, and the big flies crawled greedily about him.

Chapter 23

Stan left his scootering garments in the hall, and he and Rose set off through the afternoon sunshine. He was silent. She slipped her arm into his. 'You're not still worrying about that nonsense in the boat, are you?' she asked, a little teasingly.

'It wasn't nonsense,' he said. 'It was symbolic of my whole way of life.'

She stopped dead. 'Oh, don't be such a fool,' she said, angrily. 'We all do idiotic things at times. But we don't all brood over them for weeks afterwards.'

'I'm sorry,' he said stiffly. And she thought with misery, oh, Lord, now I've really done it.

But at that moment he said, 'What's that?'

She followed his gaze. 'It's an old quarry,' she said. 'It's – '

'No,' he said. 'There,' pointing down into the undergrowth at the entrance to the quarry.

She looked; and saw a boy's leg sticking horribly out of the nettles. But Stan was already pulling aside the nettles. 'Rose, don't come any nearer,' he called. 'It's your nephew.'

But she was already beside him, gazing with horror at a bloody, still, and twisted Gaylord. 'He – isn't – dead, is he?' she asked incredulously.

But Stan was already frantically busy, tearing off his own shirt and binding it tightly round Gaylord's upper arm. And while he worked he said in clipped, commanding tones, 'No, he's not dead. But he's been badly beaten up. Go home and get an ambulance here as fast as you can. Then come back.'

'Yes,' she said. 'Yes, Stan,' and hurried off. The sight of blood had made her sick and faint, but she forced herself to run down the lane, up the drive and into the house. The only person she met was Jocelyn. She saw the look of ludicrous surprise on his face. 'It's Gaylord,' she gasped. 'He's hurt. The old quarry.'

The colour drained from his features. 'But –' he said. 'But –'

She was already at the telephone. For a moment Jocelyn watched her helplessly. Then he ran out of the house, and did not stop till he reached the quarry.

Stan was there, guarding the unconscious Gaylord. He had found running water, and had cleaned away some of the blood with the remainder of his shirt. Jocelyn looked at his son. He had never before seen the result of personal violence. The sight of the small bruised face filled him with emotions of pity and anger such as he had never before experienced.

'Will he be all right?' he heard himself ask.

'So far as I can tell, yes,' said Stan. 'But I'm not a doctor.'

Jocelyn squatted down, took his son's hand. 'Thanks, anyway,' he said. 'Thanks for what you've done.'

Stan said, almost to himself, 'The world's a vile place. Who would want to do this to a boy?'

'You're right.' Jocelyn was surprised to hear the bitterness in his own voice. It was a sound he was not used to. 'The world is a vile place.'

The scent of honeysuckle was heavy on the warm air, and the leaves were green and tranquil against the summer sky.

Quick footsteps were coming down the lane. Jocelyn looked up. It was May, with Rose. She looked at Jocelyn as though he were a stranger. Then she went down on her knees beside her son, and took his head in her lap. 'I shall kill someone for this,' she said quietly.

Then it was evening. Gaylord was in hospital, choosing between life and death. The house was now full of police as well as relations. Jocelyn felt as though he were sleepwalking. No one could really have done that to Gaylord. It was – unthinkable. Then he was aware that someone was speaking to him. He tried to concentrate. It was May. His wife. Gaylord's mother. 'What did you say?' he asked, looking at her foolishly.

She put a hand on his sleeve. 'I said, "We're off, darling."' He made a great mental effort. Then, suddenly: 'Good Lord. You mean – ?'

She nodded.

He ran her to the nursing home, and came away alone. No May. No Gaylord.

But now, perhaps, in his loneliness he could think, which he had not been able to do since it had happened. Let him see this thing against the background of his life and beliefs. Let him gather together all the threads. An old woman dead, a young woman in travail.

A God in heaven, the loveliness of summer, a child hurt almost to death. Sunlight, starlight, laughter, the love of gentle hearts; fang, beak and claw, a pitiful mess of feathers scattered in May morning beauty.

Where was the answer? He didn't know. Somewhere, perhaps just beyond the edge of consciousness, it was all as clear as daylight. One day he would achieve the breakthrough, pierce that last barrier of the mind. But not now. Not now.

Stan said to Rose, 'I think if it's all right with you I shall stay in the village tonight. I feel I must know about Gaylord before I – go back home.'

'Oh, do,' she said. 'Look. We can't possibly put you up, I'm afraid; but come and have breakfast with us.'

He looked delighted. 'Well, if you're sure – '

So he came for breakfast. And in the middle of the meal Jocelyn walked in, looking as though he had been up all night, and said, 'May's had a girl. And Gaylord is conscious and demanding food. I've seen all – three. Both my pretty chickens and their dam.' He laughed rather unsteadily, sat down, and began quietly to cry.

Later he took Rose and Stan on one side and said, 'You know, Grebbie, you saved Gaylord's life. I – simply don't know what to say.'

At first Stan looked as though he were going to cry, he was so moved. Then he began to look more and more delighted, until there seemed a real danger that he might burst with pride. But he said modestly, 'It's just that first aid happens to be my hobby.'

'You did. You really did, Stan,' cried Rose, gazing at him as though he were the most wonderful creature that had ever lived.

Jocelyn said, 'I could offer you half my kingdom if I had one. Or my daughter's hand in marriage, if she were not still rather young.'

Then Stan went very red, and swallowed, and smiled, and looked grave, and stammered, 'You could offer me your sister's, Mr Pentecost.'

Jocelyn was still working this out when Rose cried delightedly, 'Stan,' and flung herself into his arms.

And as she clung there, laughing, she thought how strange it was that Gaylord, for whom she had never much cared, should have given Stan Grebbie sufficient confidence to propose.

Chapter 24

It was one of those perfect late summer days, the day of the funeral. The sky was hazy and cloudless, the trees still, the air breathless. You saw the countryside through a fine gauze. Every outline was softened, every cloud mellowed. It was no day for shutting anyone away out of the sunlight. But it had to be.

The lovely day faded into lovely evening. Somewhere, behind the hill, a dog barked. There was the distant clatter of milk churns. Far across the valley, a white puff of smoke from a train. In the lane, a child was singing. The child's voice was sweet and clear, completely tuneless; innocent and happy. Hearing it, Poppa felt a great sadness, though he could not have said why. Because the carefree song of a child must so soon end? Because, hearing it, he heard the song of his own lost innocence? Because there was in the house an old man who would sing no more?

He found his father in the study. He said, 'It's a pleasant evening. I thought you might care for a stroll, Father.'

The old man looked at him. 'Yes,' he said, struggling to his feet. 'Yes. Kind of you, Jocelyn.'

They set off, following the tops of the low cliffs that fringed the river valley. They were as silent as the still evening. But Jocelyn saw that his father was taking it all in; snuffing the gentle air like an animal, treading the sweet earth with a firm, loving step, while his eyes turned time and again to where the sun was going down to meet the white pockets of mist in the water meadows. Then, at last, he paused, leaning on his stick, and watched the red ball of the sun sink into the earth. He watched the warm pinks and blues, the cool greens fade from the sky. He watched the new-minted evening star throbbing brilliantly against the clear, empty blue. Jocelyn watched with him. Then, at last, the old man turned away. 'A good show, Jocelyn,' he said.

'Yes.'

John Pentecost began to walk home. His son went with him. And for once the old man seemed to be groping for words. 'A good show,' he said again. 'Is there – would you say – anything behind it all? Is it – just something we have learnt to think beautiful or – is it an expression of – something – some love, some divine caring?'

Jocelyn walked on. 'I don't know,' he said at last, 'I *think* I believe that what we've just seen is a glimpse of the hem of a garment. But – I don't know. I just don't know.'

'It could be They are simply mocking us,' said the old man.

'Mocking us?'

'The splendour of the sunset. When really – the only reality – the worms and the wet clay.'

They walked on. Below them the river writhed in its valley like a silver snake. About their heads the stars were lit one by one. By the time they reached the lights of the farm it was quite dark, and the sky wore the Milky Way across its bosom like the ribbon of an order. The old man stood looking upwards. Then he led the way indoors; turned to face his son. 'Thanks, Jocelyn. That was good of you.' He concentrated on putting his stick into the hall stand. 'I shall miss your aunt, you know. First your mother. Then her.' He gave one of his rare smiles. 'My turn next.'

Jocelyn said gently, 'Are you afraid?'

His father shot him a quick glance. 'No. No. I'm not afraid. But, you know. I shall miss it all, Jocelyn. I shall miss the earth under my feet and the wind in my mouth and the sun on my forehead.'

He took a step upstairs. Jocelyn said, 'Good night. Father. I hope you sleep well.' It was a long time, he thought, since he and his father had been so close. But the old man's defences were down. The tree was beginning to rock.

He switched the light on over his desk. He pulled out a clean sheet of paper, and sat for a long time, thinking of many things; of Rose and her love, and Becky and her love; of the old man gazing hungrily at one more sunset from his dwindling store; of May as he had seen her in the small hours of Christmas morning, with all he hoped of heaven in her smile; of the tuneless song of the little boy in the lane; of the darkness that stretched from this pool of light to beyond the wanderings of the farthest star; of Aunt Marigold, poor little woman, going off alone on the darkest journey of all; of Gaylord; most of all of Gaylord, who had learnt so soon the insensate violence of our times.

It was midnight when he finally put out the light. And he had written only four lines.

And they were not for publication.

May, tidying her husband's desk weeks later, found the quarto sheet, with the four lines set out like a poem in the middle.

Beyond the lamplight, the stars.
Beyond the sunset, the wings of the seraphim.
Beyond the face of violence, the face of love.
Beyond the face of the loved one, the face of God.

She went and found Jocelyn. He was in the barn, chopping wood. 'Did you write this?' she asked.

He looked. 'Yes.'

She sat down on the chopping block. 'Do you believe it? In spite of what happened to Gaylord and – everything?'

'Yes,' he said. 'That's why I wrote it down.' He looked at her, and smiled. 'Do *you* believe it?' he asked.

'If you do,' she said. 'Yes. Such is my faith in you, Jocelyn.'

'Thanks,' he said. He ran his finger along the blade of the axe. 'I may be wrong, of course. But – I thought about it.'

'I thought about it, too,' she said. 'When I saw Aunt Marigold. When I saw – Gaylord. But I needed you to make up my mind for me.'

Chapter 25

That was a majestic autumn. It had everything. Mornings with the white mist turning the whole valley into a saucer of milk; still, hot, honey-golden noons; afternoons so quiet that the plopping of horse-chestnuts into the grass was the only sound; evenings when the golden pumpkin of a moon grinned down on dewy-bedded lovers, and the watchful, bright-eyed mouse, and the sure-winged owl. Days when the cattle stood, tail-swishing and content, knee deep in the shallows of the river. And the dank, decaying smell of the river mingled with the harsh smell of the nettles to produce a scent that Gaylord would remember all his days.

For Gaylord had come home. A little paler, a little slower, a trifle listless. But he made up for any physical weaknesses by the bounciness of his ego. Poppa had been terribly un-forthcoming about the facts; nevertheless Gaylord had managed to piece quite a few bits together, and when facts were not available his imagination had sprung into the breach. There was the gratifying fact that the police had been round the house and the quarry like flies. The Foggerties were under the severe displeasure of the law, and it was Gaylord's opinion that they would all go to prison for years and years and years. And lastly there was the deliciously exciting fact that the Foggerty boot had torn such a gash in his arm that his life had ebbed almost away. And it had, so

Gaylord's imagination told him, taken the devoted efforts of the entire hospital staff to pull him back.

He had another reason for bounciness. He had a kid sister, someone younger than himself. He was no longer the lowest form of life known to the family.

'Can I see it?' he asked, as soon as they arrived home. But he inspected the newcomer without enthusiasm. The word sister had conjured up something with pigtails and a skipping-rope. Not, at any rate, this wrinkled and ageless thing. 'It hasn't got much hair,' he said. 'Are you sure it's a girl?'

'Quite sure,' said Momma.

That was just like her, of course. Never any doubts. But Gaylord decided to reserve judgement. It wouldn't surprise him if this turned out to be a boy, after all, cocksure though Momma might be.

But Poppa said very gravely, 'She's your responsibility as well as ours, Gaylord. You'll have to cherish her, and come between her and all harm.'

This was all very well, thought Gaylord. No one had thought to ask him whether he wanted a sister. Oh, no. And now, of course, they were asking him to share their responsibilities.

'I think I'll go out now,' he said.

'Can I come?' asked Poppa.

'Yes, of course,' said Gaylord magnanimously. They went out into the sunshine. Poppa said, 'Let's go to the top meadow and sit in the sun.'

They set off. Gaylord felt very mature, very assured. It was a nice change having someone younger than oneself about the place. Perhaps Momma would treat him with a bit more respect now.

They climbed the stile into the top meadow. Gaylord lay down, knees asprawl, while his father sat cross-legged on the turf and went through the pleasant ritual of filling and lighting his pipe. Then, putting his matches back in his pocket he found an apple and threw it to his son.

Jocelyn puffed his pipe, and felt the sun burning deliciously into his cheeks and bare forearms. The murmur of the bees was as sweet as their honey. Sounds of happy munchings came from Gaylord, drowsing through the long, hot afternoon of childhood. Jocelyn felt a strange lightness of the spirit, almost as though he were standing outside himself, reviewing the situation of this Jocelyn Pentecost. He looked at his son, sprawled in the sunlight with the utter abandon of youth, one bare arm across his eyes, his strong teeth tearing into the flesh of the apple.

He's going to be all right, thought Jocelyn. His body's healed, and it's not done anything to his mind, thank God, unless it's made him a bit more cocky. And if he can get over this, he should manage most of the hurdles life has to offer. And what, wondered Jocelyn, will he make of life? Well, at least he'll be an individualist. He'll plant his feet firmly on the ground, and take the rough with the smooth, and be moderately truthful and a little more honest than most. Yes, he thought proudly, he'll be a sturdy, decent man with a streak of obstinacy and a mind of his own; all of which he'll get from his mother, not from me, poor fool.

He stood up, put a hand on Gaylord's sun-hot knee. 'So long,' he said. 'I must get back to your mother.'

'So long,' said Gaylord. He looked up, and his black eyes were grave with all the responsibilities of elder brother. Then he grinned; and he was once more that most content of all creatures – a little boy, eating an apple in the sunlight, under an English heaven.

Eric Malpass

Beefy Jones

Beefy Jones is a lovable rogue. Not very bright, but strong and kind-hearted, he lives with a gang of petty criminals and Jack-the-Lads in the disused loft of the church hall in Dandy. The vicar, meanwhile, is blissfully unaware of this motley gang of uninvited occupants. Returning home early one evening, Beefy overhears a meeting of the Church Council where under discussion is the demolition of the church hall – their home. The gang then embarks on a series of adventures with one aim in mind – to sabotage the vicar's plans by any means they can in order to save their home. In this hugely funny and intriguing story, they find themselves plunged into a series of wild, madcap escapades with the willing, naïve Beefy always at the centre of the action.

The Lamplight and the Stars

Nathan Cranswick's third child comes into the world on the day of Queen Victoria's Diamond Jubilee. Whilst the Empire celebrates, Nathan's concerns are about his family's future. A gentle and wise preacher, he gratefully accepts the chance to move from the dingy, cramped house in Ingerby to the village of Moreland when he is offered a job on the splendid Heron estate. Anticipating peace and tranquillity for his wife and young family, his hopes are cruelly dashed when their new life is beset by problems from the beginning. A family scandal and the Boer War menace their whole future, but finally it is the agonising choice facing his gentle daughter which threatens to tear the family apart...

Eric Malpass

Of Human Frailty
A biographical novel of Thomas Cranmer

Thomas Cranmer is a gentle, unassuming scholar when a chance meeting sweeps him away from the security and tranquillity of Cambridge to the harsh magnificence of Henry VIII's court. As a supporter of Henry he soon rises to prominence as Archbishop of Canterbury.

Eric Malpass paints a fascinating picture of Reformation England and its prominent figures: the brilliant, charismatic but utterly ruthless Henry VIII, the exquisite but scheming Anne Boleyn and the fanatical Mary Tudor.

But it is the paradoxical Thomas Cranmer who dominates the story. A tormented man, he is torn between valour and cowardice; a man with a loving heart who finds himself hated by many; and a man of God who makes the terrifying discovery that he must suffer and die for his beliefs. Thomas Cranmer is a man of simple virtue, whose only fault is his all too human frailty.

ERIC MALPASS

THE RAISING OF LAZARUS PIKE

Lazarus Pike (1820–1899), author of *Lady Emily's Decision*, lies buried in the churchyard of Ill Boding. And there he would have remained, in obscurity and undisturbed, had it not been for a series of remarkable coincidences. A discovery sets in motion a campaign to republish his works and to reinstate Lazarus Pike as a giant of Victorian literature. This is a cause of bitter wrangling between the two factions that emerge. For some, Lazarus is a simple schoolmaster, devoted to his beautiful wife, Corinda. For others, who think his reputation needs a sexy, contemporary twist, he is a wife murderer with a deeply flawed character. What follows is a knowing and wry look at the world of literary make-overs and the heritage industry in a hilarious story that brings fame and tragedy to an unsuspecting moorland village.

SWEET WILL

William Shakespeare is just eighteen when he marries Anne Hathaway, eight years his senior. Anne, who bears a son soon after the marriage, is plain and not particularly bright – but her love for Will is undeniable. Talented and fiercely ambitious, Will's scintillating genius soon makes him the toast of Elizabethan London. While he basks in the flattery his great reputation affords him, Anne lives a lonely life in Stratford, far away from the glittering world of her husband.

This highly evocative account of the life of the young William Shakespeare begins the trilogy which continues with *The Cleopatra Boy* and concludes with *A House of Women*.

Eric Malpass

The Wind Brings Up the Rain

It is a perfect summer's day in August 1914. Yet even as Nell and her friends enjoy a blissful picnic by the river, the storm clouds of war are gathering over Europe. Very soon this idyll is to be swept away by the conflict that will take millions of men to their deaths.

After the war, the widowed Nell leads a wretched existence, caring for her husband's elderly, ungrateful parents, with only her son, Benbow, for companionship and support. But Nell is a passionate woman and wants to share her life with a man who will return her love. Meanwhile, Benbow falls in love with a German girl, Ulrike – until she is enticed home by the resurgent Germany.

This moving story of a Midlands family in the interwar years is a compelling tale of personal triumph and disappointment, set against the background of the hideous destruction of war.

928262

Printed in Great Britain by
Amazon.co.uk, Ltd.,
Marston Gate.